TOO SWEET

Copyright © 2025 by Abby Millsaps

All rights reserved.

paperback ISBN: 9798988800392

No portion of this book may be reproduced, distributed, or transmitted in any form without written permission from the author, except by a reviewer who may quote brief passages in a book review.

This book is a work of fiction. Any resemblance to any person, living or dead, or any events or occurrences, is purely coincidental. The characters and story lines are created by the author's imagination and are used fictitiously.

Copyediting and Proofreading by VB Edits
Cover Design © Silver at Bitter Sage Designs

Contents

Dedication	V
Content Warning	1
Blurb	3
1. Locke	5
2. Joey	13
3. Joey	19
4. Kylian	25
5. Locke	29
6. Joey	32
7. Decker	37
8. Joey	41
9. Decker	49
10. Joey	55
11. Locke	59
12. Joey	63
13. Locke	69

14.	Kendrick	73
15.	Joey	81
16.	Joey	85
17.	Kylian	91
18.	Decker	95
19.	Josephine	99
Afterword and Acknowledgments		113
Also By Abby Millsaps		115
About The Author		117

To the readers who just can't get enough of the Boys of Lake Chapel. I love you more than Decker loves rules—more than Nicky loves philosophy—more than Kendrick loves spoiling his woman—and more than Stats Daddy loves Sunday mornings.

This one is for you.

Content Warning

Too Sweet contains content some may find triggering, including a descriptive recollection of past abuse and child neglect, explicit language, Daddy kink, breath play, and characters living in pain because of chronic illness.

Blurb

Life has been nonstop since the day I became Mrs. Crusade. Not that I have any interest in slowing down now that I've found my rhythm in Lake Chapel.

I love my life, my boys, and the future we're creating together.

This semester, I even get to live with my best friend and her cohort of men.

There's more than enough room at the Crusade Mansion for the ten of us, but between conflicting schedules, increased security measures, and Kendrick's NFL draft intentions, it's rare that I get time with all four of my guys.

That's why I'm thrilled about our plans for Valentine's Day.

Spending an entire weekend off the grid with the men I love is my personal version of heaven. I'm craving quality time with each of them (and hoping for some quality group fun, too).

All I want for Valentine's Day is to be snuggled up at the cabin with Kylian, Locke, Kendrick, and Decker.

But apparently, my guys have other plans.

When it becomes clear they've uncovered a secret I intended to keep to myself, I'm forced to face the reality of what it means to be loved by four possessive, overbearing men.

Chapter 1
Locke

"Dude. I've been looking for you everywhere."

Kylian doesn't look up right away—clearly intent on finishing what he's working on before giving me his attention. The dining room table has disappeared under piles of papers, folders, monitors, and tablets.

I shift from hip to hip and cross my arms over my chest. The move makes the healing skin on my back pull slightly. I'm still sore as fuck after spending four hours in the tattoo chair last week.

It'll be worth it.

I can't fight my grin as I think about her reaction. I've been counting down the days until February fourteenth. I can't wait to get away and to spend time with my girl and all the boys this weekend.

"Congratulations." Finally, Kylian shifts papers off to one side, then, bringing his hands together in front of him, peers up at me through his thick-framed glasses.

Cocking my pierced eyebrow, I wait for him to continue.

"You located me. Mission accomplished. Well done, you."

I bark out a laugh. "*Well done, you.* Seriously? You're spending way too much time with the Brit."

Kylian raises both eyebrows in concession, the slightest hint of a smirk teasing the corner of his mouth.

"Perhaps. But Jo is happy, and Hunter is safe." He surveys the table, then blows out a long breath. "Or at least as safe as she can be with Magnolia still alive."

Eyes narrowed, I give him a once over. He looks tired yet determined. Resolute yet somehow wary, too. I'm worried about him. He's working too hard.

His word choice also concerns me. Kylian always says what he means, and he means what he says. Aside from the occasional joke, or a rare moment where he's masking in front of others in a social setting, it's safe to assume he's being literal. Magnolia, Hunter's mom, is terminally ill, but is he implying that she *won't* be alive soon?

Hunter and her men moved into the mansion over winter break, then Decker insisted they stay for the semester. It's worked out well for the most part, but I'm stoked to get away this weekend, just the five of us. We're heading up to the cabin for Valentine's Day. And I missed the hell out of Joey last weekend when she went to the Combine with Kendrick. We need this time away.

Despite living in a literal mansion, the house has felt cramped lately. Hunter's boys love the gym, and the Brit keeps the oddest hours. Honestly, I'm not sure if the guy sleeps at all. Then there was that incident when I walked in on Mrs. Lansbury and Spence's butler guy having a private moment in the pantry.

I shudder involuntarily at the memory.

"What's up?" he asks, jolting me from my thoughts.

With a sigh, I put my concern to rest. I trust Kylian. Kylian trusts Spence. Hunter is Joey's best friend. When Joey was the one in danger, then when Joey needed to be avenged, Greedy didn't hesitate to roll up his sleeves and get his hands dirty right alongside Kendrick and Cap.

"Just wanted to check in with you about this weekend. See if you needed any help or if you wanted me to pack for you."

Kylian's been grinding harder than usual, which is saying something, because the guy works all the time as it is. Between school, his stats analyst work for the Lake Chapel football team, and now helping with increased security and whatever Spence has him mixed up in, I figured he might need some extra help.

"I'm already packed," he declares, pushing away from the table. "I'm waiting on one more order, but it's being delivered to the cabin and appears to be en route with a confirmed delivery of tomorrow. Otherwise, I'm ready to go."

"Nice. What'd you get her?" I rub my hands together, trying to ease some of the soreness in my knuckles.

Living with chronic pain is a bitch. This flare-up is mild, but I want to stay on top of things before we head to the cabin. I'm planning an ice bath tonight, followed by a soak. If the hot tub's unoccupied. Another downside of living with five extra people this semester? Hunter's guys make liberal use of all the amenities.

"I did not *get* Jo anything," Kylian replies. "I curated an experience she will find equal parts amusing and sexually satisfying."

I balk. "Sexually satisfying? I thought we were testing out the cock ring attachment together?"

This particular vibrating cock ring has an adjustable part that I can anchor to my pubic piercing. Kylian found it online and is excited about the ability to sync it to his phone. When he presented the idea to me last month—with a fully prepared deck—I was instantly on board. So was Kendrick. I'm down to try anything once. Especially if it pleases our girl.

"This is something separate," he says. "Something I have planned for Jo tomorrow afternoon, when we arrive."

Unease settles in my chest. I'm not jealous, exactly. But I always feel a little off-kilter when it comes to navigating shit like this. I want Joey to have time with each of my brothers, no doubt. But I can't help but worry that whatever Kylian has planned doesn't upstage what I did for her for Valentine's Day.

"Nicky."

Head snapping up, I meet my best friend's gaze. I don't bother trying to hide the apprehension coursing through me. Kylian may not be great at reading social cues most of the time, but he knows my deepest worries and darkest secrets. I can't hide shit from him.

"Statistically speaking, Jo's going to thoroughly enjoy the cock ring. But your other gift? She's going to absolutely love it. It's top tier."

I release a breath I was very aware I was holding, thanks to the ache in my ribs and the burning sensation behind my sternum. "Right. Yeah, you're right. Thanks, man." I run one hand through my hair, then take another steadying breath. "What time do we leave again?"

He waves me over. "Here." He hands me one of the iPads from the table, then reaches for another for himself. I watch the screen as he mirrors the devices and taps on the itinerary he created.

But before his schedule loads, the master calendar app catches my eye.

I home in on the calendar listing for Saturday, February fourteenth. There's a line indicating we'll be at the cabin. Another line that lists Valentine's Day. Then below that, there's a third line. Two words. Eleven letters. I count them as I read it, over and over again.

Jo's Birthday

My pulse pounds in my head as the screen changes. The itinerary appears, but those two little words dance across my vision, taunting me and making my brain glitch so badly I can barely make sense of what I just saw.

"Go back," I grit out. Tension has coiled in all my muscles. Anxiety is percolating in my gut.

Kylian looks up, bewildered. "I didn't even go forward yet."

"No. Kyl. To the calendar. Go back to the calendar."

I'm gripping the sides of the iPad so tightly I'm afraid it'll crack in my hands. This can't be happening. This can't be right.

But then again...

I have no fucking idea when Jo's birthday actually is.

The calendar reappears.

"There." I stab at the words. "It says Jo's birthday right there. Is that for real?"

Kylian scowls. "Of course it's for real. Why would I add something not real to my master calendar?"

The fuck? I glare at him, breaths sawing in and out of my lungs.

"How long have you known?" I make an effort to unclench my fists. The last thing I need is to cause myself even more pain ahead of this weekend.

"Known what?" Kylian asks.

He's not being obtuse, and he's not fucking with me. He needs me to spell it out for him—to make it black and white. It takes every ounce of my patience to keep it together.

With a cleansing breath, I try again.

"How long have you known that February fourteenth is not only Valentine's Day, but *Joey's birthday*?"

Kylian squints one eye, considering. "Since September third."

"Motherfucker." I rake both hands through my hair. February fourteenth is this weekend. That means Joey's birthday is literally two days away.

Another realization slams into me.

"Do Cap and Kendrick know?"

With a huff, Kylian glares up through his glasses. "I assume they do not. To my knowledge, Jo has never shared her birthday with any of us."

"God dammit." I drop the device on the table and whip out my phone. "We've got to get them down here. Emergency meeting. Right here, right now."

I text the others, telling them to meet us in the dining room ASAP.

When I look up again, Kylian is watching me. With a steady gaze that takes concerted effort on his part, he maintains eye contact. "Did you consider that if Jo hasn't mentioned her birthday before now, there's a strong probability she does not want to acknowledge the day?"

Shit. I had not.

Decker bursts into the dining room with Kendrick hot on his heels.

"What's wrong?" Decker demands, looking from me to Kylian, then back to me again.

His intensity fuels me. My concern isn't unwarranted. If Joey's birthday is this weekend, that's a big fucking deal.

"Locke. What is it?" Decker presses.

I blow out another breath, then raise both eyebrows and tip my chin to Kylian. "Daddy Genius over here has something he forgot to share with us."

Kyl rises to his feet, sets down the iPad, and folds his arms over his chest. "Or I happen to possess information that's not mine to share."

He and I stare at each other, our silent stand-off raising the tension already sizzling around the room. He has to tell them. It's not okay for two of us to have this information and the other two to be kept in the dark. We're a team. She's *our* girl. All of us. I'm not backing down on this. Decker and Kendrick have a right to know.

"Spit it out." Kendrick splays his hands wide on the table, clearly trying his best to keep it together as we all wait out Kylian. "Your text said this was urgent, and about Jojo. Don't leave us hanging."

Sighing, Kylian gives me one last incredulous look. Then he turns to the others and finally clues them in.

"Nicky's all worked up because he was looking at my calendar and saw that Jo's birthday is coming up."

Decker's face falls. I swear I see the exhale leave his body. "Seriously? When is it?"

I wait a breath. Then another. Kylian's being exceedingly difficult, so I come out and say it. "It's Saturday. *This* Saturday. Joey's birthday is on Valentine's Day."

There's a single moment of silence, then Decker and Kendrick simultaneously explode.

"Are you for real? That's only two days away."

"How the fuck did I not know it's my wife's birthday this weekend?"

My thoughts exactly.

A deluge of relief washes over me. Decker and Kendrick get it. This is a big fucking deal, and we've got work to do.

"How long have you known?" Kendrick grumbles, the question aimed at Kyl.

"Since September third," he repeats, clearly annoyed by everyone's reactions.

The others stride over, looking equal parts agitated and anxious. Decker and Kendrick look the way I feel right now: like we dodged a bullet, but just barely.

I breathe another sigh of relief. That was close. We almost fucked up big time. I'm just grateful we realized how important this weekend really is before we head up to the cabin.

We wanted to make our first Valentine's Day special. Now that we know it's Joey's birthday? We're going to make this a weekend she won't ever forget.

Chapter 2
Joey

The change in vibration through the floor of the SUV is the first sign that we're close. If the road has turned to gravel, that means we're minutes away from pulling up to the cabin.

I'm so jazzed I could bounce right out of my seat—except Kylian wouldn't allow that to happen under any circumstance. I'm securely buckled, and he's got his arm pressed across both my legs, gripping my upper thigh as he scrolls on his phone with his free hand.

I lean back as much as the seat belt and Kylian will allow, brushing my hand up Nicky's arm and squeezing.

"We're almost here," I tell him in a gleeful whisper.

He leans forward from the bench, hitting me with his megawatt smile. "You excited, Hot Girl?"

I can't temper my responding grin. Excited is an understatement. I'm thrilled to be getting away with all four of my guys for a weekend of rest, relaxation, and hopefully a lot of fucking.

"I can't wait." I take his hand and kiss his tattooed knuckles. "How are you feeling?" I ask, trying to keep my tone light.

Nicky's arthritis has been well-managed over the last month or so. He did take an ice bath last night, though, which always makes me worry that he's flaring. Because honestly, who would willingly submerge themselves in an enormous tub filled with bone-chilling water?

"I feel good right now." He shifts his neck from side to side, then stretches his arms overhead, checking for any new aches. "I'll feel even better when we're unpacked and I'm buried deep inside you."

My body warms in response to the hungry look in his eyes.

"We're two minutes out," Kylian murmurs. "You both need to remain seated—and clothed—until the vehicle comes to a complete stop."

I roll my lips to keep from snickering. It's usually Decker who's over the top about safety.

"Relax, Daddy Genius," Nicky quips. "I can wait. I'm fully committed to seeing all our plans through this weekend."

My heart skips a beat. "Plans?" I ask, looking between my guys. "What kind of plans?"

"Hey now," Kendrick calls from the driver's seat. "Don't be giving away any of our surprises."

My giddiness ramps up another ten notches. Surprises? As in more than one?

Leaning forward, I grip Kendrick's shoulders. "How about a hint, big guy?"

He meets my gaze in the rear-view mirror, his smoldering stare possessing the same ravenous look he hit me with every time we were alone last weekend at the Combine.

As a shiver rolls through me, I bite down on my lip and hold his gaze.

"You're trouble, Mama," he mutters. He glances away and puts the SUV in reverse so he can park it as close to the cabin as possible.

In the passenger seat, Decker turns at the waist and assesses me up and down. "When did you eat last, Josephine?"

I fight my instinct to sass back. It used to be my go-to response when it came to my grump of a husband. Apparently old habits die hard.

"I had a late breakfast," I assure him.

Decker's obsidian eyes narrow as he sees right through my hollow reply.

"And what did you eat?"

With the slightest of eye rolls, I avert my gaze and fiddle with my seat belt. Kylian reacts instantly, covering my hand with his and preventing me from unbuckling before the vehicle is fully stopped.

"Toast."

"*Just* toast, Josephine?"

I blow out an aggravated breath, making my long bangs flutter around my face.

"Yes, just toast. Would it make you feel better if I lied and said it had some sort of nut butter on it, Cap?"

His answering scowl tells me no; no, it would not.

"We're here," Kendrick declares, momentarily saving me from my husband's interrogation.

With a renewed jubilance, I unbuckle and hop out of the car. Nicky follows out my door, but before he can reach for me, Kendrick has already captured me in a hug, his arms slung low on my hips.

Nicky mutters something about getting the bags from the trunk and leaves us to it.

I peer up at K, inhaling deeply, savoring the scent of fresh mountain air combined with the hints of musk and vanilla that are uniquely him.

"Sure you don't want to clue me in to these surprises?" I lick my lips, craning up so I'm just inches from his face.

Grinning, he pulls me in tighter and buries his face in my neck. "You're trouble," he repeats. "But you're also my favorite fucking prize. I love you, Jojo. I love you so goddamn much."

His lips find my neck, the stubble on his face tickling me until I'm squirming in his arms.

"But you better go make nice with your husband before we have an extra grumpy Cap on our hands." He pulls back and swats my ass playfully, then heads around the side of the vehicle to help unload.

K's right. Riling up Decker is my favorite pastime, but I don't want there to be an ounce of tension or grouchiness this weekend. It's rare we all get to be alone together nowadays. We have to make the most of it while we can.

It's been an adjustment having Hunter and her guys at the house. I'm so damn grateful Decker insisted they stay all semester, but I can't pretend it's all rainbows and sunshine on the Crusade Isle.

I thought living with my bestie would mean uninterrupted girl time and nonstop fun. I was very, very wrong.

Our school schedules and Hunter's class load make it hard to find time to just hang. Add in the eight moody, overprotective men we're also sharing space with. Not to mention the still evolving dynamic of Hunter's group as her guys get to know each other and figure out how to work together. Then there's the Bad Mood Brit to consider.

It feels like there's always something going on at home nowadays. I don't mind the full house, and I relish knowing that my best friend is as safe as she can be given the circumstances. But this weekend brings with it a highly anticipated break for me and my guys. I intend to make the most of it.

I catch up to Decker on the porch where he's punching the code into the keypad. A quick shiver rolls through me as we wait.

He side-eyes me and sighs as the lock unlatches. "It's too cold out here to not be wearing a jacket, Siren."

I wrap both hands around his sweatshirt-clad arm—we're all wearing sweats and hoodies, but I don't bother pointing that out to him—and pop up onto my toes to kiss his cheek.

"Then I guess you better get me inside and warm me up, Cap."

The slightest hint of a smile teases at one side of his mouth. In the next second, he's scooping me up, bridal-style, and carrying me over the threshold.

"I'll crank up the heat and turn on the fireplace," he promises, flicking lights on with his elbow as we journey farther into the cabin. "Then I have to get dinner started." He sets me down on one of the oversized leather couches in the middle of the great room.

Grinning, I shift forward to hop up and help him, but his signature Decker scowl freezes me in place.

"Sit and let me take care of you, woman." He waits for me to obey.

I make him sweat it out for a few seconds, then with a cheeky grin, I settle back against the couch and cross my legs underneath me.

Settling into the cushions, I inhale deeply, taking it all in. The cabin has become such a special place for me... for all of us, really.

Although my first trip here was under duress, we've come back a few times since. Those stays have easily made up for the visit when Decker and I weren't together (his choice) and I unexpectedly found myself agreeing to marry him (my choice).

This place isn't just peaceful, it's significant to each of us in lots of ways. Kylian is less connected to the outside world out here. We both sleep so soundly and deeply in the Den. Kendrick finds peace walking quietly through the woods. Decker makes a concerted effort not to let work and school and all his other obligations get in the way when we're here. Even Nicky says he physically feels better at the cabin: something about the fresh air and the barometric pressure.

Above all else, we all feel safe in this place. This cabin feels more like home than any place I've ever resided. Even more so than our house on the isle. I love that we came up here for Valentine's Day weekend. I can't wait to spend more holidays in our own private sanctuary.

I watch as Decker moves around the room, adjusting the thermostat and using a remote to set the gas fireplace blazing.

He snags two blankets off the ottoman before making his way back to me. Then he takes a knee, covers my lap with both blankets, and takes my hands in his, interlacing our fingers.

His gaze settles on the rings on our left hands for a moment. Then his dark, steely eyes travel up to meet mine.

"One minute," he requests on a shaky breath.

Heart stuttering, I quickly nod.

One minute, when it's just him and me...

Neither of us says anything for a beat. He bends forward, kissing my forehead and brushing a few stray hairs away from my face. I revel in the contentment settling around us. His steadiness and comfort are as grounding as the cabin itself.

After the full minute passes, I murmur, "Thank you for loving me so well."

He grasps my face in his hands, then kisses me deeply and reverently, but pulls back before it can build to anything more.

"Always, Siren. Through every storm. I live and breathe for you, Josephine."

My breath catches, and my heart does riotous somersaults in my chest. I'm so affected by his words and proximity. I'm also desperate for more.

I pull him back down to me, feeling all sorts of needy. Growly and grouchy or surly and serious are Decker's go-to modes. But soft and sweet Decker gets me every time.

"Come here," I urge, trying to pull him onto the couch—or, more accurately, onto *me*.

Groaning, he shakes his head. He pecks me on the lips once more, then rises to stand. "I have to get dinner started. Otherwise it won't be ready until midnight. That's why I asked about what you've eaten today." He scratches the back of his neck, gazing down. "Dinner won't be ready for several hours... I just wanted to make sure you eat something now if you're hungry."

I hold my hands out, and Decker takes them, pulling me off the couch.

"I love you." I push up on tiptoes, but he still has to bend to kiss me once more. "I'll grab a snack, then I think I'm going to take a nap."

Stifling a yawn with the back of one hand, I keep hold of Decker as he guides me toward the kitchen.

I can hear the others joking around, probably getting things unloaded from the car and unpacked in the kitchen.

It feels like my heart is floating in my chest as the sounds of their banter, joy, and laughter follow me through the cabin.

Chapter 3
Joey

The deep sedation of sleep has me so drowsy I can barely open my eyes. I have no idea how long I've been napping. I suspect a few hours, given how sated I feel. I'm relaxed from my scalp to my toes.

I let myself roll around the enormous bed—an upgrade to the primary suite we made over the holidays—stretching out all my limbs and savoring the delicious chill of the sheets.

The crisp coolness won't last, so I'll enjoy it now while I can. Tonight, with any luck, I'll have multiple men warming this bed.

When I finally crack my eyelids open, I'm startled to see a glowing blue light from the corner of the room.

It only takes my brain a few seconds to catch up. Kylian. Sitting in the dark. Scrolling on his phone. And now that I'm awake, staring right back at me.

"It's creepy to watch people sleep." I sit up against the headboard and pull the blankets with me so they're tucked under my chin.

Kylian sets the device down, but keeps the screen pointed up, presumably so we can still see each other.

"I've watched you sleep almost every night since we've been together," he states.

"What?" I laugh. "No way."

"Yes way," he counters. "Every night we've been apart since we got together. Except for last weekend. I tried to convince K to stay on the phone after we were done with virtual phone sex, but he refused. He claimed the light would bother you while you slept."

My cheeks heat at the memories of last weekend. Kendrick and I were at the NFL Scouting Combine. After we celebrated his amazing performance in the hotel shower, we FaceTimed the other guys and let them celebrate with us, too.

"Why?" I ask. My voice is soft and breathy.

He rises from the chair and stalks toward me, backlit by the illumination from his phone. He's exquisite in the blue light, his handsome face and high cheekbones accentuated by the glow and sharp angles of his glasses.

When he's beside the bed, he grips my chin and tips my head back slightly.

"I watch you because I'm obsessed with you. Every breath you take, I want to witness. Each little sigh in your sleep, I want to hear. Every smile. Every grimace. I want to see them all. I need to remember them. Commit them to memory."

He leans forward and dusts his lips over mine.

"I watch you because I like the reminder—and the reassurance—that you're mine."

Heat flares in his bright blue eyes.

Sparks of arousal ignite in my chest.

He angles in closer, his lips ghosting over mine in a mischievous smile.

"Are you ready for your first surprise, baby?"

Giddiness replaces the lust pumping through my veins.

"Yes!" I slap my hands to the mattress, ready to hop out of bed and get on with it.

But Kylian doesn't move. He doesn't even let go of my chin. Instead, he nips my bottom lip and says, "Yes, what?"

Another shiver rolls through me, sparks of excitement and stimulation illuminating my insides once more.

"Yes, Daddy."

With an approving smirk, he straightens and pulls me to my feet. "Good girl. Let's go."

Rather than lead me out of the room, he guides me through the dark to the en suite bathroom.

As soon as he pushes open the door, my senses are overwhelmed by the scents of sugar, vanilla, and buttercream. The lights are turned low, and there are lit candles on every surface.

But the pièce de résistance is the tub.

The enormous, deep, white porcelain tub that's filled with more sprinkles than I've ever seen in one place.

I bring both hands to my mouth, absolutely shocked by the sight before me.

The tub isn't just partially full, and I don't see any water. I think he actually filled the entire basin with multicolored sprinkles.

My cheeks burn from smiling as I take it all in.

"You didn't," I finally say, biting my bottom lip as I look over to meet his gaze.

Puzzled, he looks from the tub then back to me. "Clearly, I did."

My brilliant, literal boy.

I squeeze his neck, bouncing on my toes like a little kid. "Please tell me we're getting in."

His pointed look zaps all the excitement I was just feeling.

"Baby. Under no circumstances could I possibly get into that tub."

Okay, fair. Just looking at that many sprinkles all in one place is overstimulating. I can't imagine what it would actually feel like. Although I really do want to find out.

"You, however?" His salacious grin is my first clue. "You are going to strip naked, climb into the tub, and then be the very best girl for me by using this on your clit."

One brow cocked, he reaches toward the vanity and procures an enormous wand vibrator.

I scurry to undress, smiling like a fool as I rip off my clothes. I pile all my hair on top of my head, hastily secure it with the elastic around my wrist, then pop one hip for good measure.

"How do I look?"

Kylian assesses me up and down, then shamelessly adjusts his erection.

"Like you want to sink into 834.6 pounds of sprinkles and grind against this wand until you come so hard you see stars."

I'm on him a second later.

Our kisses are frantic. Desperate and needy. He grips my hip hard, shifting back just enough to work the vibrator between our bodies.

When he turns it on, I moan and hitch one leg around him, trying in vain to get even closer.

"Get in the tub," he commands against my mouth.

I whine, not wanting to leave him or the source of the heat that's already building low in my belly.

"Jo."

He clicks the vibrator off.

I deflate. "Not fair!"

With his hands on my upper arms, he guides me over to the tub. "Be a good girl and do what I say. *Now.*"

I wiggle my ass against him. "Yes, Daddy."

Stepping into the tub of sprinkles is unlike anything I've ever experienced. At first it tickles, but as I settle in, it feels like a million gentle pinpricks. My skin warms instantly as my body reacts to the sensation. It's not uncomfortable, just wildly foreign. Like all my senses have been turned up. Like I'm primed and extra perceptive to every touch.

My ass doesn't even touch the porcelain, making me feel like I'm floating on a cloud. I giggle again. I can't help it. It's a heady experience, being absolutely sheathed in sugar. The sweet scent wafting up around me is so strong I can practically taste it.

Grinning up at Kylian, I reach for the vibrator. "I don't know if this is going to work—"

"Oh, it'll work. I've been fantasizing about this for days, baby. Sit back. Relax. Spread your legs and put this right where you need it. I can't wait to watch you come over and over again, surrounded by sprinkles."

Chapter 4
Kylian

She's a vision. The star of every erotic fantasy I've ever conjured. The center of my world, the holder of my heart, and the keeper of my peace.

Based on the flush on her neck and chest and the pitch of the moans she's making, she's also very close to climaxing. Again.

I'm right there with her, as if my pleasure aims to align itself with hers.

The primal need to mark her—to connect in this moment—urges me forward.

However, every inch of skin from her chin to her toes is submerged in sprinkles and inaccessible to me right now, including her hands.

I can tell by the way she's curled forward that she's double-fisting the wand as she grinds it against her core.

"Look at you, baby. Working so hard to make yourself come again. Such a good fucking girl, making a mess with all these sprinkles."

Surprisingly, my words have the opposite effect of what I intended.

Panting, Jo flops back, all the tension snapping out of her body.

"Daddy," she whines. "I can't. It's too much. There's too many."

In fairness, she's working toward her third orgasm. Her hairline has accumulated a sheen of sweat. I can only imagine the way the little sugar particles are sticking to her body. With a shudder, I force myself to focus.

"You can't?" I challenge, a clear edge to my voice. "You're giving up, just like that?"

Her brow furrows. "I need—"

I bend low and capture her lips in a kiss, feeding my tongue into her mouth over and over. "Get on your knees and straddle the vibrator."

I pull back to give her enough room to reposition.

She moves slowly at first, then eventually settles in. A rainbow of sugar shifts around her with each movement. Once she's got the wand between her legs, I grip her shoulder and press down.

She gasps on contact.

"Wider," I encourage, gently squeezing her neck as she does what I say.

Her pupils dilate, her focus entirely set on me.

"Good girl," I murmur, checking to make sure she's still with me. I squeeze her neck harder, trying to drive her higher. "Grind on it, baby. I want you to have this. I want you to come again, and if you're a very good girl, Daddy will come, too."

Her whimper tells me I've hit my mark.

"Harder, Jo. I'm getting close."

That's an understatement. I've been painfully close to coming this whole time. But if my girl needs a bit of motivation, I'm more than capable of obliging.

Her breathing turns to pants. One of her hands emerges from the tub, delicate fingers circling my wrist.

"More," she manages to croak. "Fucking choke me, Daddy."

A feral growl rips out of my chest. I squeeze her throat harder. Jerk my cock faster. And watch with reverent admiration as her face reddens, her eyes flutter closed, and she topples over the edge one more time.

She screams, then curses. A single tear escapes the corner of her eye.

I release my grip on her throat as she peaks, but I keep my hand resting against her skin so she knows I'm right here. When I'm sure she's through the thick of it, I drag my thumb across her bottom lip.

Her eyelids drift open, her gaze glassy and unfocused as she comes down from that high.

"You did so well, baby. You deserve a reward. Stick out your tongue."

I bring my cock to her lips, jerking myself until I'm careening over the edge. My entire lower half seizes, the pleasure blooming all the way up my legs and through my length as jets of cum shoot out of my cock and coat her tongue.

"Hold it," I grunt.

I milk my cock until it's empty, ensuring every last drop lands in her mouth. It's a voluminous load, and a bit starts dribbling down her chin. I catch it with one finger and paint it over her lips.

Then, with my other hand, I reach down, pinch a few sprinkles between my fingers, and scatter them all over her cum-coated tongue.

"Now you can swallow."

She does with a grin and a satisfied groan.

"Thank you, Daddy."

I bend low and kiss her once more, savoring the combination of salty and sweet still coating her tongue. When I pull back, I cup her cheeks in my hands, covering the rest of her face with kisses. "You're perfect, baby. So fucking perfect for me."

Chapter 5
Locke

I barely tasted my dinner. Hardly remember asking Cap if he wanted help with the dishes. I've been trying to contain my next-level excitement all damn day leading up to what we have planned for tonight.

An app-controlled adjustable cock ring is secured snuggly around the base of my shaft, with the vibrating extensions of each end of the device twisted around my pubic piercing.

"You doing okay there, brother?" Kendrick smirks as he pulls off his shirt.

I close my eyes and squeeze the end of my dick, trying to calm the fuck down after our dress rehearsal.

Doing okay, I am not. Barely holding on is more like it.

I insisted I could get the cock ring situated all on my own.

That didn't stop Kylian from testing out each of the settings once it was secured in place.

Now it feels like my dick has been supercharged. Joey hasn't even joined us yet, and I'm fighting back telltale tingles of pleasure.

I steady my breathing and think about Heraclitus. He's my least favorite philosopher, mostly because the dude would have been content to just set things on fire and chalk up the ensuing chaos to the ever-changing state of the universe.

Fuck. Okay. Crisis averted.

Glancing around, I let myself focus on what we're about to do. The room is covered in candles, their soft glow comically romantic in contrast to the filthy group sex that's about to commence.

Kylian and K have their shirts and pants off, standing at the end of the bed in their underwear. My lower half is bare, but I'm keeping my shirt on for now, hoping to hold out a little longer when it comes to my surprise. With any luck, what's about to happen will be so fucking hot Joey won't notice.

When the bathroom door cracks open, the three of us whip our heads in her direction.

She emerges in a hot pink set—satin ribbons and frilly lace tied up over her hips and tits. My mouth waters on instinct.

"Hot Girl," I groan. I fight like hell against the urge to get up and go to her. The only thing stopping me is the perfectly positioned cock ring secured around my manhood.

"Oh my god. What is that?"

I smirk. Leave it to Joey to sweep across the entire room and instantly home in on the new sex toy.

"One of your surprises," Kylian offers. "It's an adjustable cock ring that I special-ordered to enhance the experience of external stimulation when you grind on Nicky."

Joey looks aghast. "Does it hurt?"

Kendrick sidles up behind her, laughing. He slides his hands up and down her lingerie-clad hips.

I track the movement, aching to touch her, too.

"Does he look like he's suffering, Mama?"

I fight back a grin. My cock's fully erect and leaking precum from the tip. If this is suffering, sign me up for a lifetime of torture.

"Get up here, Hot Girl," I encourage.

She climbs onto the bed, then drops to hands and knees and fucking crawls to me. Every lithe movement of her body ratchets up the anticipation burning inside me. Behind her, Kendrick and Kylian are just as transfixed by our woman as I am.

She's gorgeous. A fantasy come to life. She's perfect, and she's all fucking ours.

I'm more determined than ever to create a night she'll never forget, starting right fucking now.

Chapter 6

Joey

"Pull her."

Nicky groans. I whimper.

This is the edging from hell. I've never been hornier.

Before I can form words and properly object, large hands grip my hips and lift me away. Despite how my inner walls desperately clench around Nicky's cock, I'm no match for Kendrick's strength or Kylian's authoritative instructions.

"No, no, no," I cry out, pounding my fists into the mattress.

K grips my hips, pulls my ass into the air, and slides all the way into me in one thrust.

"Fuck. Yes," I moan at the pleasure that comes with the new angle.

I'm a mess. A needy fucking mess. I'm desperate for release and will clearly take anything I can get.

Chuckling, Kendrick fucks into me at a lazy pace. I push back faster, grinding my ass as best I can, desperate for him to go deeper.

"I need more," I plead, first looking back at him, then setting my pouty gaze on Kylian.

"I know what you need, Mama," K soothes. He runs one palm up my spine, then lets his fingertips trail down the same path until he reaches my ass. With a firm squeeze on one side, he gives me a decent spank on the other.

Arousal surges through me. Another moan escapes.

"But right now, all I can give you is what Daddy Genius will allow."

My head snaps around to where Kylian's standing off to the side, his phone securely fixed in his hand. Rather than staring at the screen like I expected, he's fixated directly on me.

"Daddy," I whine. "Please."

His blue eyes blaze with desire, the heat behind his stare so intense I feel it like a sharp smack against my clit.

"Please," I beg, my desperation getting the best of me.

"She's dripping back here," K remarks.

Kylian shoots him an unimpressed glance. "Guess you better clean her up."

With a few steps forward, he gets close enough to lean over the bed and catch my mouth in a hot, wet kiss.

"Crawl forward, baby. I want you to deep throat Nicky while K eats you from behind."

I scramble to comply, stretching forward and taking Nicky as far back in my throat as I can manage.

"Easy," Kylian growls, gathering up enough of my hair and twisting it around his wrist to control my movements. "Savor him, baby. Taste yourself on his cock and show him how much you love this."

Kylian guides my head back down as I lap at Nicky's length. I run my tongue up and down his shaft with each gentle tug of my hair.

"Fuck. Fuck. Fuckity fuck," Nicky pants. "I'm gonna fucking blow."

"No you're not," Kylian says.

The tension of my ponytail leash loosens. When I glance over, he's using his phone to change the settings of the cock ring.

"*Fuck*," Nicky grinds out through clenched teeth, the tendons in his neck straining.

His cock fills more of my mouth. When I open my eyes, it looks like the base of the ring is inflating. Angry veins throb up and down his length.

He's aching for me just the way I am for him. I double down, swirling my tongue around his crown and making a mess on his dick.

"She likes that," Kendrick reports. "She's so fucking aroused I can't lap her up fast enough."

Kylian tugs on my hair hard enough to pull me off Nicky's shaft. I whimper, then school my expression when I see the devilish smile on Kylian's face.

"You're being such a good girl for us, baby. Are you ready to come now?"

Tears accumulate in my eyes at the promise of release.

"Yes, Daddy. Thank you, Daddy."

"Lick Nicky's cock goodbye," Kylian quips, guiding my head once more and pressing me down as low as I can go.

When I gag, he holds me there, forcing me to swallow past the fullness and breathe through my nose.

"Such a good fucking girl," he growls, pulling my hair until I'm upright, then kissing me on the mouth.

When he pulls away, he smirks, that mischievous glint in his eye telling me he's not done with any of us just yet.

"Back up and let Nicky take you from behind, baby. Nicky—you stay sitting just like that."

Kylian tips his chin at Kendrick, who's peering up from between my legs.

"Switch with me," he says. "She loved tasting herself on Nicky. Time for her to clean you up, too."

Everyone moves quickly, the tension coursing through the room so thick I feel like I can't even take a full breath.

Once I'm straddling Nicky backward with K off to my side, Kylian climbs onto the bed.

"Here." He thrusts one hand forward, holding out a bottle of lube. "Coat your piercing and the extensions of the cock ring. I want you to line it up so you can slip into her ass."

Cold liquid slides between my cheeks. I moan when Nicky pushes one finger past my puckered hole.

"Fuck," he grunts in my ear. "I can feel myself inside you, Hot Girl. Hottest fucking moment of my life."

Kylian hooks each one of my legs on the outside of Nicky's. Then he presses my hips back, picks up his phone, and fucking sends me to the stratosphere when he activates the vibrations of the cock ring.

Nicky slips his finger out of my back door and lines me up just like Kylian instructed.

Kendrick steps forward, gripping his cock and guiding it to my lips with a grin. "Open, Mama. Let's fill up all these holes."

I open wide, stretching around him the best I can.

My pussy flutters around Nicky's cock, the stretch even more intense from this angle. Vibrations start low in my core. The sensation of the toy pressed up against my tight bundle of muscles has my cunt spasming with every roll of Nicky's hips.

I'm climbing higher and higher but trying so damn hard not to get my hopes up.

I squeeze my inner walls and hollow my cheeks.

I'm about to close my eyes when another sensation distracts me and nearly tips me over the edge.

Popping off K's dick, I look down and find Kylian smirking up at me through his glasses. Just the very tip of his tongue flicks against my clit, but it's enough. More than enough. It's everything, and I'm about to fucking explode.

Even more eager, if possible, I work K's length, licking and sucking.

"That's it, baby. Right there. This is how you're coming. This is how you're all fucking coming."

He hovers.

I hold my breath.

Kendrick groans.

Nicky begs.

"Such a good girl for us, baby. Such a good fucking girl. You're so perfect. As soon as I put my mouth on you and latch on, you're going to come for us, understand?"

And then Kylian cranks up the vibrator to the highest setting and simultaneously closes his mouth and teeth around my clit, sucking so hard I careen forward and freefall into a warm, wet, never-ending abyss.

Chapter 7
Decker

I quietly hover over the pile of them, trying to gauge who may actually still be awake. The room is warm and smells like sex. It also smells like frosting. I wrinkle my nose, confirming I made the right call by relegating myself to the kitchen tonight.

Kendrick's eyes meet mine through the dark. The others appear to be asleep. He holds my gaze, goading me for not joining them tonight, I'm sure. Then, in silent understanding, he slinks his arm out from under Josephine's head. I tip my chin appreciatively, leaning forward and running both my hands up her bare thighs.

"Josephine," I murmur. I keep my voice low, hoping not to wake Locke or Kylian.

She stirs, then sleepily groans, flops onto her stomach, and hooks one leg around Kendrick's lower half.

This is going to be harder than I thought.

The repressed rumbling through K's chest shakes Josephine's body, but she still doesn't stir. I circle around to his side of the bed. Crouching, I brush the back of my knuckles against her cheek.

"Josephine. Wake up."

"Go away," she grumbles.

Kendrick is officially losing it—laughing so hard she's being dislodged with each shake of his chest.

Annoyed, I take matters into my own hands.

I reach out and lift my wife's body effortlessly, tucking her into my chest.

"Shh," I soothe before she can protest. "I want to take you somewhere, Siren. It's a surprise."

She cracks one eye open and searches my face, then sighs and rests her cheek against the fabric of my henley. "It better be a good surprise, Cap. It's late and I'm boneless after—"

"Hush." This time, the shushing comes out more insistent. I bow down and kiss her, effectively cutting her off. I don't need a full recap of all the reasons she's currently boneless.

My possessiveness has been on a steady simmer since the day I fell for this woman. Sharing her with my brothers has been an experiment in tolerance, patience, and introspection.

Not a day passes that I don't feel the hot jabs of jealousy over our dynamic.

And yet I couldn't imagine it any other way.

Josephine is happy. My boys are thriving.

If the occasional possessive spike is the price I have to pay to have her in my life, I can learn to live with that. I can, I will, and I do.

The promise that Josephine will always make time for me—even if it's one minute—is what galvanizes my attitude and warms me from the inside.

I've figured out when I need to excuse myself—like tonight—and when I need to get over myself and join in the fun. It makes her so damn happy to have all of us together. The high she feels from "full group activities" puts and extra pep in her step for days.

I'll never deprive her of that joy. Hell, I'll never deprive her of anything. Her happiness is my purpose. The desire to make her laugh or to see her smile fuels me in a way football and accolades never could.

"Let's get you dressed," I murmur, shifting her in my arms and grabbing for her overnight bag. "You'll need layers and a jacket. It's cold tonight."

Her head pops up with interest. "We're going *outside*? Why?"

"You'll see." I place her gently on her feet. "The faster you get dressed, the faster you'll get your next surprise." I gently swat at her ass.

She grins at me over her shoulder, then scurries to the bathroom. But before she closes the door, she turns and shows me her bare backside, giving a little shake of her hips. She catches my gaze and winks—then promptly closes the door.

This girl.

My wife.

"This seems like cruel and unusual punishment, Cap."

I smirk but pull her closer to my side, hoping she's not too cold for what I have planned. I've been working on this idea since Christmas. I even came up to the cabin earlier in the week to ensure everything was set up to my standards.

We trudge along the path, which is well lit with the solar-powered lights I had installed.

Josephine shivers, and I silently curse myself for not insisting she add more layers. I didn't want the bulk to be uncomfortable, though.

"Almost there," I promise.

It's her turn to scoff. Blue eyes glare up at me, her skepticism clear on her face. Before she can offer up her signature sass, a branch snaps farther along the trail to the left.

I switch positions and tuck my wife into my other side, squinting into the darkness and listening intently. The rustling of leaves and the sound of a scampering ease my concern.

"We're okay. It's something small, like squirrels or maybe a fox chasing a rabbit."

Josephine peers up again, her gaze sweeping down to where I have my hand shoved in one pocket of my jacket.

"And yet you're still gripping the bear spray in your pocket?"

I force my grasp on the can to loosen, but I don't let go of it completely. The bears in this area should still be deep in hibernation. *Should* being the operative word. I'll never take chances where protecting her is concerned.

My answering scowl delights her, just like it always does. Josephine pulls the knit beanie off her head and tosses it to me, forcing me to release my grip and catch it, just like she knew my instincts would require me to do.

She tauntingly takes a few steps backward, her eyes dancing with mirth.

I jog up to catch her, then sling my free arm around her shoulders, planting a kiss on her forehead and securing the hat back in place. "I thought you were cold, Mrs. Crusade?"

She grins up at me, then settles back into my side as we continue along the path.

Chapter 8

Joey

We come upon a clearing, and I don't know where to look first. The inky black night sky is punctuated by dozens of stars and wispy clouds, but it's the setup in front of me that takes my breath away.

A warm glow from the solar-powered lights along the ground is mirrored by strands of twinkle lights draped between posts. The little glimmers of illumination surround a shiny, perfectly smooth surface, the glassy area in sharp contrast to the dark brush that covers most of the forest floor.

I whip my head around to gauge Decker's reaction—only to meet his obsidian gaze and realize he's solely focused on me.

A beat of silence passes. When he raises both eyebrows expectantly, I finally string together a coherent thought.

"What is this?" I whisper. I look back to the clearing, wondering if perhaps I'm dreaming.

Decker grips my hand, guiding me a few steps forward.

"It's an ice-skating rink. I made it for you."

I halt, causing Decker to rebound back. Red creeps up his neck and flushes his cheeks in the most uncharacteristic way. I nearly lose my balance, and I'm not even standing on ice yet.

"You made this—for me?"

Decker's jaw ticks, but he nods. "It's Valentine's Day weekend, Josephine." He pauses, lips pursing like he's resisting the urge to say something else. With a quick shake of his head, he adds, "I wanted to do something special for you."

I snort, then hold out one arm. "We could have watched a movie, Cap. Instead, you built me an ice rink?"

When and how did he have time to do this?

He closes the space between us, tipping my chin up with two fingers. "There isn't anything I wouldn't do to be the one responsible for the look on your face right now."

Tenderly, he bends low, placing a soft kiss on my lips.

"You deserve every happiness, Josephine. My life's purpose is to figure out new ways to make you smile."

Giddiness whooshes through me as I let his words sink in. I can't believe he did this. It's over-the-top and extravagant and yet so sweet and unassuming. I'm so enchanted I feel unsteady on my feet.

The second I think it, I sway forward. Although, of course, Decker doesn't let me fall. With a firm grasp on both my arms, he ensures I'm stable before capturing my lips and kissing me again.

Love drunk.

Decker Crusade has officially made me love drunk.

"Wait." I look over to the rink, then tilt my head back to meet his gaze. Our exhalations dance together to form little clouds. Watching the wisps swirl between us reminds me that we're standing out in the cold. I'm warm from the inside, filled with so much love I can hardly sort through it all.

"Is that some sort of lake or pond?" I don't remember there being a body of water here. I catch my lip between my teeth, eyeing the smooth surface of the ice with a bit more skepticism this time. It's cold, but it's not *that* cold. *Little Women* (Winona's Version) is one of my comfort movies. I'm not about to pull an Amy and slip into icy waters.

With the pad of his thumb, Decker releases my bottom lip from between my teeth.

"Do you really think I would ever allow you to skate on a frozen body of water, Siren?"

Both my eyebrows shoot up in defiance. Husband or not, this man doesn't *allow* me to do anything.

He catches on quickly and corrects himself a second later.

"I didn't mean allow. I just meant…" He swipes a hand through his hair, agitated. "Come this way." He guides me toward a bench along the frozen surface. Beside it, there's a large outdoor storage container that looks like something where firewood might be stored. Decker nods toward the bench, and I sit. Then he pulls out his phone and opens up an app.

"There's a cooling element and liner at the base of the rink. All five inches of water are frozen solid. Kylian made sure I can monitor and adjust the temperature from my phone. There's no natural water source underneath the ice because I would *never* put you in that kind of danger. I came out here earlier to make sure everything was set. I've been working on this since Christmas, and I've got it all down to a science."

Okay then.

That only leaves me with one last concern.

Worrying my lip, I peer up at my husband once more. He did all this for me—and it's romantic and so thoughtful—but there's a good chance it might all be in vain.

"I've never ice-skated before," I admit quietly.

Decker's face softens with the confession. He kneels before me, then takes both my gloved hands in his.

"Do you want to try? I think you'll enjoy it. And I promise I won't let you fall."

His subtle vote of confidence is all I need.

"I'll try it," I confirm with a nod.

He opens the storage trunk and procures two pairs of ice skates. Both pairs are black and clunky—more like rollerblades than the pretty white ice skates I was envisioning.

He must notice the look of confusion on my face. Holding them up, he explains, "Hockey skates. These have more ankle support and are easier to learn on."

Then he proceeds to ease my boots off one at a time and lace up the skates. Once he's checked the lip and tightened the laces—twice—he gets to work putting on his own set.

He stands with ease, positioning himself in front of me and offering both hands.

I give myself a little pep talk, then let Decker help me to my feet. Stumbling immediately, I cling to his forearms and curse under my breath.

"You're okay," he murmurs.

I meet his gaze and seethe when it registers that he's on the brink of laughing at me.

"You just have to get your bearings. Come on. Once we're on the ice, it'll be easier."

Easier, it is not.

This is ridiculous. Nothing about it is fun. I'm taking choppy little baby steps like the ice has personally offended me while desperately clinging to my husband. My ankles hurt, and my thighs are burning. What about this is supposed to be fun, exactly?

"Okay, let's try something else," he finally suggests.

I would side-eye him if I wasn't so afraid of throwing myself off balance. "Unless that something else is sitting down, I'm not particularly interested."

He's come to a full stop in the middle of the rink, meaning I'm not moving anymore either. "Steady on your skates," he instructs.

With a deep breath, I find my balance. That doesn't stop me from squirming and digging my gloved hands into Decker's arms.

"Okay, now loosen your death grip and hold my hands."

My eyes shoot up to his. Like hell am I going to loosen anything right now.

This time he doesn't bother holding in his laughter. "You can do this, Siren. You're making it harder on yourself by clinging to me."

"I thought you liked it when I'm clingy," I quip.

He raises both eyebrows and offers a hum of contentment. "You're not wrong. But I want you to prove to yourself that you can do this."

With a groan, I blow a few stray hairs out of my eyes.

Decker's gaze narrows, his mind working overtime. Then he straightens a fraction, like something has clicked.

"Actually, I want you to prove to *me* that you can do this. Come on, Josephine. Show me what you've got."

A fire lights inside me.

Ugh.

It's a natural response. Truly second nature. Leave it to Decker to motivate me with a challenge.

"Okay," I huff out. "I can do this."

I gingerly work my hold on him lower, pausing when I have his wrists in my hands, then pushing forward until my hands are resting on top of his upturned palms.

He curls his fingers, and I follow suit so we're locked together, even if he has almost no grip on me.

"Bend your knees, baby. Eyes on me. Here we go."

Before I can object, he glides backward. How he can skate backward is absolutely beyond me.

I focus on his face, just like he asked, and try to keep my knees loose as I let his momentum carry me forward.

The urge to squeeze my eyes closed is strong. But Decker holds my gaze, his animated expression dishing out assurances and praise that keep me going.

"Hold on," he murmurs.

That's all the warning I get before we're turning—oh gosh, it's a sharp turn—whipping along one side of the rink.

"Decker!" I scream. Though I feel like I'm falling, our momentum keeps me upright.

His laughter rings out through the night. "I've got you," he assures me for the dozenth time.

He pulls me all the way across the rink, and this time, it's not quite so scary.

Then he circles us around again. And again. And again.

Cold air whips around us, but all I see, all I feel, all I care about is the warmth blossoming inside me at this moment.

I'm doing it. I'm really doing it.

Laughing, I tip my head back as far as I dare without throwing myself off balance. The stars above us twinkle like they're in on this secret. The lights strung around the rink dance in my periphery, their glow an exact match for the effervescent lightness warming me from the inside out.

For every heartache and hardship, we've persevered and come out stronger.

For every hurdle we've just barely cleared over the few months we've had together, we've survived and come out steadier.

There's not a single doubt in my heart or mind that this man loves me to the very core of who I am. I feel it in the way he looks at me. In the way he cares for me. In the way he nurtures my spirit, builds me up, and puts in the work every single day.

"One more minute," Decker warns.

My thighs are burning, I'm cold down to the very marrow of my bones, and I can feel my heartbeat in my throat. But despite the way my body protests, I don't want to stop. I could stay out here forever, him and I.

I'll never forget this night. I'll never take for granted the way this man loves me so well.

On the final lap, Decker holds my gaze, the question clear in his eyes.

I catch my lip between my teeth, unsure.

"You've got this, Siren," he encourages, giving me one of his rare megawatt smiles.

With a quick exhale and a subtle nod, I consent.

I've got this.

And even if I don't, Decker's right there. He won't let me fall.

With the slowest of movements, almost like he's caressing my palm instead of letting go, he releases me. I have enough momentum that I glide forward several feet. He skates faster, leaving more space between us for me to close all on my own.

Gracelessly, I slam into him to stop. We're both laughing as we try to stay upright.

"You did it," he praises, rubbing his cold nose against the length of my jaw. The contact sends a shiver through me, his icy exterior in juxtaposition with my flushed face.

"I did it," I whisper in disbelief.

Decker guides me over to the bench and helps me sit, then makes quick work of removing my skates. Before he can stand, I scoot forward, wrapping my arms around him and burrowing my face into his neck.

"I loved this," I confess, sincerity drenching my every word.

"I love you," he replies. He swaps out his skates and pulls me to my feet. "Let's get you inside, Siren. It's late, and you've got to be freezing."

I don't comment, because I honestly don't mind. As much as I griped about the weather on our way out here, every single second of this experience was worth it.

On the journey back up to the cabin, I wrap my arms around his bicep. "Do you think we'll have another chance to come out here this weekend?"

He gives me a satisfied smile. "Possibly."

"Oh! What if the guys come too?" I wonder if there are enough skates for everyone.

"That's a less likely scenario," Decker hedges.

Before I can ask why, he goes on.

"Kylian hates ice-skating. I'm sure he can present a whole diatribe as to why. Locke might be amenable, but he's in really good shape now and hasn't had a flare up for weeks."

Shit. I should have thought of that.

"K can't risk injury ahead of the draft."

Damn. Should have thought of that too.

"Besides," Decker adds, softer now. "I was hoping maybe this could be our thing."

My heart floats in my chest. I cuddle up closer, hold my husband a little tighter.

Our thing.

I love the sound of that. Just like I love living life with this man.

Chapter 9
Decker

It's late when we finally get back to the cabin. My instinct is to head to bed, but there's a quieter part of me that never wants this night to end. I've always done the right thing, made the responsible choice. Tonight, I want to go for what I crave, no holds barred.

"Do you want to warm up together in front of the fire?" I ask as we strip off our outer layers.

Her cheeks are bright pink, flushed from the cold and the exhilaration of skating.

Bending over to remove one boot, I steel myself for disappointment. It's late. I'm cold and already sore. She must be freezing. Maybe it's better if we both just call it a night and head to bed.

Her answering smile pierces through my chest with such intensity, I stumble trying to pull off my other boot.

"I would love that."

After I right myself, I pull my wife into my arms. She yelps when my freezing hands crawl up under the hem of her shirt and splay wide on her low back. I don't let her go; I just hold her tighter.

"You're so soft and warm," I murmur, bowing my head so I can kiss her jaw.

Josephine snickers. "Those are two words I never imagined you would use to describe me, Cap."

Shaking my head, I lead her over to the couch in front of the fireplace. I've never been more grateful to have a remote-controlled setup than I am right now. I snag the remote before we sit, then crank up the flames to the highest setting.

"Come here."

She complies without hesitation. My girl's in rare form tonight.

Pulling her into my lap, I brush all her hair to one side, then tuck my chin into the crook of her shoulder.

Josephine emits a full body sigh, relaxing back into me and letting me take more of her weight.

We sit quietly, our gaze focused on the fire as the flames dance before us. Warmth eventually reaches us. Josephine relaxes into my hold even further.

She brushes her hands down my arms, linking her fingers through mine and pulling my arms around her torso.

A wave of emotion washes over me. It's contentment and joy mixed with anxiety and frustration.

I want it to always be like this with her. I want to have a lifetime of laughter and teasing, cuddling in front of the fire and holding her close.

But I'm a realist. I know this moment—where everything feels easy and perfect and oh so sweet—isn't something we can hold on to forever.

Life happens. We'll face challenges and have to overcome obstacles.

It might not always feel like this, but it's my life's mission to chase this high and give her this level of peace and contentment as often as possible.

When Josephine leans back, I can't help but readjust and pull her closer.

"You're the very best part of me," I whisper into her ear.

A shiver racks through her.

My need to care for her seizes my brain. "Baby, are you still cold?"

Wordlessly, she turns, swinging one leg over my lap so we're face to face.

"Josephine."

She doesn't answer.

Instead, she kisses me, soft and slow. Almost lazily, as if we have all the time in the world.

But that still doesn't ease my concern.

"Josephine." I pull back, and she pouts. "Answer me. Are you still cold?"

She bites down on her bottom lip, her eyes glassy, blown-out orbs peering up through her thick lashes.

"I'm freezing, Decker. But I know exactly what you can do to fix it."

Her mouth finds the tendon in my neck. She nips playfully, then licks the spot as her words settle my anxiety.

"Warm me up, husband. I need your heat."

She grips the hem of my Henley, then pulls it over my head.

Matching her languid movements, I gather the fabric of her shirt and do the same.

Her chest rises and falls in rapid breaths. My eyes track the movement as she reaches both hands behind her and removes her bra.

I keep my gaze focused on her face as she shimmies off my lap. Rising to her feet, she quickly unbuttons her jeans and steps out of them.

She's bare before me, her silhouette framed by the licks of flames behind her.

She's exquisite in every sense of the word. She's warmth and goodness and everything I've ever wanted—for myself, and for my brothers.

I shove down my pants and boxers, desperate to feel her heat where I crave her most.

She climbs back onto the couch, spreading her legs to straddle my lap. My hands caress along the curve of her hips, guiding her closer and welcoming her home.

She hovers just out of reach, the sweet heat from her core teasing the tip of my cock.

"Let me have you, Siren," I practically growl.

She rests her forehead against mine and closes her eyes, then uses one hand to grip me and put me right where she wants me. She takes her time lowering down, her warmth consuming me as she takes inch after inch until I'm fully sheathed.

With a shuddering breath, she opens her eyes and stares right into my soul. "You have me, Decker. I belong to you." Then, with an uncharacteristic softness I never get from this woman, she whispers, "Please keep me. And never let me go."

I smash my mouth to hers, thrusting up in the same breath. I pour everything I am into the kiss. Tasting her. Devouring her. Giving and receiving until our mouths meld into one and we're connected as deeply as possible.

Breaking away, I fuck up into her again, holding her against me. "I dare someone to try and take you from me," I rasp into her ear. "Let them fucking try."

She kisses my neck, rolling her hips.

Every time she thrusts forward, I feel the tug in my core. Every time she sheaths me with her warmth and goodness, I have to grind my molars to keep myself from coming first.

Everything she does—everything she is—it's all so sweet.

Her lips hover inches from mine, our breaths mingling and our foreheads pressed together. I finally loosen my grip and caress her skin. I trail my hands up and down her back, then circle them around and brush my fingertips against her nipples.

"More," she murmurs, the sharp points of her nails digging into my shoulders.

I roll her nipples between my forefingers and thumbs, matching the movements to the deep, soul-shifting drive of our lower halves.

She's getting close—and thank fuck for that, because I'm tensing every muscle in my body to stave off my own release.

I move one hand to her hair, cradling the back of her head, and snake my other hand between our bodies, bringing my thumb to her clit and rubbing her in quick, tight circles.

When her heat clenches, I know this is it. She unravels beautifully, her head thrown back in ecstasy as her body pulls me deeper and tugs at the very essence of who I am. It's the sensation of her letting go that finally unleashes my release.

Waves of pleasure ripple through me, the sweetness of the moment washing over me and fortifying everything I feel for this woman.

As we come down, neither one of us makes any moves to separate.

I'm so satisfied. So content. So utterly blissed out that I can't imagine anything I want or need more than my wife in my arms.

Wordlessly, I stand up, taking care to keep us connected. I arrange a few pillows, then lie back down on the couch, pulling an oversized blanket over our bodies.

Josephine nuzzles into my neck, kisses the hollow of my throat, and whispers, "I love you" before falling asleep in my arms.

Chapter 10
Joey

The first thing I notice when I crack open my eyes is just how dark it is. My mind fogs in confusion. It has to be morning. After a few blinks, the dots start connecting in my mind. I'm not out in the living room anymore. I'm downstairs in the Den.

Expectantly, I reach over, but all I find is an empty bed. I scan my surroundings and see that my phone has been plugged in to the charger on the nightstand. When I lift it to check the time, I'm shocked to see that it's almost noon. I ignore the date on the screen—it's just another day—and set the device down again.

A day I'm looking forward to for once, because I get to hang out with all four of my guys. No obligations. No jaded memories. Just the five of us together.

I shoot up to sitting but instantly regret it.

My legs ache, and my stomach muscles feel like they've been put through the wringer. I'm embarrassingly sore. Especially considering I didn't do much except cling to Decker as he dragged me around the ice rink last night.

Decker.

I fell asleep in his arms in front of the fire last night. Naked, sated, and happier than I've ever been in my life.

It's that thought that spurs into action.

I'm wearing his shirt, so I leave that on and find a clean pair of sweatpants in a drawer. My toiletries bag is already in the en suite, so I take a few minutes to brush my teeth, take my meds, and swipe on deodorant and mascara. Throwing my hair into a messy bun is the final step before I leave the room and traverse the stairs.

I move stealthily up the open corridor, following the sound of my guys talking in the kitchen.

"Do you think we should wake her up?" Locke asks. He's met with a chorus of objection from the others.

Smirking, I reach the landing, then pad through the great room until all four men come into view.

Except they're not what catches my eye first.

Shit on a crumbly cracker.

There are balloons. Poorly placed streamers. An absolutely *massive* pile of stuff sitting on the table. But it's the banner strung up along the wall that confirms the rapid-fire pulsing of my heart isn't in vain.

Happy Birthday Joey.

Fuck.

There's a ringing in my ears. Little spots dance in the periphery of my vision. I feel myself slipping, falling back into a darkness I didn't even realize I was at risk of stumbling upon today.

At some point while I'm trying to steady my breathing, the guys notice my presence and swarm. I'm being passed around from one person to the next—and not in the fun way—as each of my men hugs me and wishes me a happy birthday.

By the time Decker releases me, my lungs have seized and I can't breathe.

No one seems to notice that I've gone catatonic.

I'm ushered over to the table. It feels like everyone's trying to talk at once.

There are wrapped gifts, along with several items just there on display. I spot a new Kindle and a pair of green Airpods Max headphones.

There's a super cute loungewear set I can barely stand to look at. Not because it doesn't look ridiculously soft and cozy, but because what it symbolizes.

They didn't do this at Christmas. We exchanged gifts, but everything was low-key, thoughtful, and in Kylian's case, practical.

How did this happen? And how the hell am I going to put a stop to this onslaught? They weren't even supposed to know about today.

Before I have the chance to utter a word, Kendrick is before me, opening up a jewelry box and presenting it with a flourish.

When I meet his gaze, he's grinning from ear-to-ear.

They all are.

Shit.

Not only is this my literal nightmare, but now I'm about to be the bad guy.

"What is all this?" My voice comes out cold and impartial. On the inside, I'm fighting like hell to hold back tears.

Nicky steps forward. The joy emanating from him kills me.

"It's all for you, Hot Girl. We know it's your birthday. We wanted to make it extra special since it's the first time we're celebrating together."

I give up on trying to hold back tears. They fall freely as I shift my focus to resisting the urge to scream.

My stomach twists, and it feels like there's a deadweight smashing into my chest. It's too much. Too real. Too intense for me to hold inside.

I watch the scene transform before my eyes. The way their expressions change. The way the energy in the room morphs into an acrid poison.

I watch as the realization sinks in for each of them. They see it now. That I don't want this. I didn't ask for this. And that despite their sweet intentions and kindness, I can't help but feel angry.

With a forceful sniffle, I swipe the tears off my cheeks.

"I don't want to celebrate my birthday," I state plainly. My voice is shaky, but I know I have to stay true to myself. I look at each of them, making sure they hear what I say next. "I didn't ask for any of this, and you shouldn't have done it. Please get rid of it all. I'm going to go outside and get some fresh air."

With that, I grab a random half-full coffee mug off the kitchen island, snag a blanket from the living room, and turn my back on my guys.

Chapter 11
Locke

"Need I remind you—"

"I know," I snap, cutting Kylian off at the pass. I fucking know. Or at least I know now.

"What the hell was that all about?" Kendrick snarls. He looks from me to Kylian, then glances over to a bewildered Decker. "Did something happen last night?"

Decker holds up both hands in surrender. "No. Everything was great."

Kylian crosses his arms over his chest and sighs. When no one says anything, he finally puts us out of our misery. "Clearly, she did not want any of us to acknowledge that today is her birthday."

"She's my fucking wife!" Decker hollers. He rakes both hands through his hair, mussing up the strands so they're sticking up in every direction.

"She can't really expect us to act like today is no big deal," Kendrick adds. He's shaking his head, gripping the edges of the table where Joey's unwanted presents mock us.

"We fucked up," I huff, clenching my fists, then unclenching them just as quickly when jolts of pain shoot through my knuckles. I take a deep breath and blow it out slowly, trying to get a grip.

Decker stomps toward me, but then turns before he reaches my side and takes off in the other direction. He's pacing the length of the table, and he makes a solid ten passes before he finally speaks again. "I'm not going to ignore her birthday for the rest of our lives."

I want to agree with him. But then I think about the devastated look on Joey's face just now.

Kendrick matches Kylian's stance and tips his chin toward the other man. "You look smug as fuck. And don't think I didn't notice you didn't add any presents to this pile. Help us make sense of this, Daddy Genius. What'd we do wrong?"

Kylian locks eyes with Kendrick. "Simply put? Everything."

Decker emits a low growl. I fight the urge to upturn the damn table. I scan the contents scattered all over the surface. Now that K points out Kylian's lack of tangible gifts, I realize everything on this table is from Decker and Kendrick. They very clearly went overboard in an attempt to spoil our girl.

"It's the stuff," I say quietly, shame and frustration vying for dominance in my mind. "It's all this fucking stuff."

Decker freezes, his gaze focused squarely on me as his jaw ticks. Seething, he accuses, "You're the one who called the emergency meeting two days ago. You rallied us and made it seem like we had to go big."

Kylian holds up one hand, shaking his head at Decker.

"That's not an accurate portrayal of what occurred. Nicky alerted you to the significance of the date, yes. But you don't see a massive pile of presents from him anywhere, do you? This"—he makes a sweeping gesture around the kitchen, ending at the present-covered table—"was all your idea." He pins Decker with a glare, then shifts his gaze to Kendrick.

"She didn't react this way at Christmas. She was excited about all the surprises we had planned this weekend," Decker defends.

Kendrick whistles low. "To be fair, she thought this weekend's surprises were for Valentine's Day."

The puzzle pieces are snapping into place faster than I can process them. We fucked up so badly. I'm finally starting to see the full picture.

Kylian continues. "Christmas was a mutual gifting opportunity in which we all agreed upon a budget. That was a reciprocal experience with clearly defined guidelines. There was nothing unexpected about the exchanging of tangible items on that day."

Decker's still not backing down. "She shouldn't be surprised that we want to go all out on her birthday. We *always* give her a ton of attention. If she can't handle it because there's four of us—"

"Hey now." Kendrick holds up both hands and gives Decker a pointed look. "That's not fair. If Jojo didn't even mention her birthday to us, she clearly wasn't expecting all this. I feel like we overreacted and overwhelmed her at once."

"It's the stuff," I repeat, defeated. I should have seen this coming. Out of all of us, I'm the one who grew up rough and raised by useless excuses for parents. I should have been able to fucking identify that Joey has trauma related to her birthday.

Resolutely, I look around the room. "We have to make this right."

Chapter 12

Joey

I'm clinging to the lukewarm coffee mug like it's my last lifeline. I don't even want the putrid liquid, but holding the mug gives me something to do between texting Hunter. One timid sip confirmed what I feared—I grabbed Decker's cup in my hasty exit from the kitchen. The man rarely drinks coffee as it is, but when he does, he takes it black.

I'm not surprised when the sliding glass door creaks open and my four guys file out onto the deck.

Their crestfallen expressions and puppy dog eyes kill me. One of them looking at me that way would be enough to make me want to gloss over the whole ordeal. But when they all have the same expression and I'm the one responsible for putting it there?

Ugh times four.

I shoot off one last text to Hunter, then stash my phone away.

"Hi," I offer meekly as the guys inch closer, circling the hammock where I've made camp.

Kylian is the first to reach me. He slides onto the hammock and pulls me into his arms without hesitation.

A fraction of the tightness in my chest loosens, but most of the shame is still there. Instinctively, I rub at my breastbone. I hate feeling like this. More importantly, I hate that I made them all feel like shit, too.

"We're sorry, Hot Girl." Nicky takes my hand, interlacing our fingers. "We shouldn't have gone all out and made a big deal about your birthday without talking to you first."

I offer him a weak smile, my eyes watery with unshed tears. I don't want to make them feel worse. But I can't fight back the anxiety and anger that stir up for me on February fourteenth when there are balloons and a banner reminding me of the day.

I wanted this year to be different. Up until twenty minutes ago, I was sure it would be. Hell, for the first time in my adult life, I was excited about this day.

Nicky strokes his thumb over my hand. "We popped every balloon. We tore down the streamers and the banner. We stashed the presents away. We'll put the cake out in the trash tomorrow before we leave."

I tip my head up to meet his gaze. "There was cake?"

Kylian leans over and runs his nose along my jaw. "Vanilla buttercream with extra sprinkles."

My heartstrings tug at the thoughtfulness. They went all out. I hate that I can't just enjoy this for what it is.

"Talk to us, Mama," Kendrick encourages. "What's going on?"

Sighing, I sit up, then rise to my feet and stretch out my arms. The blanket I was cuddling under falls to the deck. Nicky tsks and whips his hoodie off over his head.

"Here," he insists, helping me put my arms through it.

I smile at him appreciatively. "Thanks." I cross my arms and steel my spine, grateful for the extra warmth. It's way too cold to be out here without some sort of layer or blanket.

"So Nicky's allowed to give you something?" Decker mocks.

My eyes flit to his face, shooting daggers at my dense-as-hell husband.

Kendrick lightly shoves him in the chest. "You just don't know when to quit, do you, Cap?"

With an exasperated exhale, I look to each of them. Then, before I lose my courage, I dive in and try to explain as quickly and succinctly as I can.

"You already know my mom was a piece of work."

My generous assessment of the woman who birthed me earns a chorus of grumbles.

"She left me home alone a lot when I was growing up, from as early as I can remember. Probably even earlier than I remember, if I'm being honest."

One of the guys growls.

I close my eyes, hold up both hands, and shake my head. "I know. *I know*. Please just let me get through this."

Gentle fingers brush the side of my face, tipping my chin back. I assume it's Nicky or Kendrick. When I open my eyes, I'm met with stoic, sincere obsidian irises. "We're listening, Siren."

Hope floats inside my chest. I can do this, and I owe it to all of them to try and explain. Squaring my shoulders and standing to full height, I continue. "She only bought groceries once a month. I learned at a young age to ration the food to make it last. Thankfully my school district had a food assistance program. I had free breakfast and lunch as long as I made it to school."

My stomach twists at the memory. "When I was in second grade, my teacher took it upon herself to reach out to my mom and ask if she wanted to provide the Valentine's Day snack for our class party since it coincided with my birthday."

The weight of the memory clogs my throat, filling my gut with dread, even all these years later. Apprehensively, I whisper, "I didn't ask the teacher to do that. I didn't even know she had called my mom until the night before."

Locke's arm snakes around my low back as he pulls me into his side. "It wasn't your fault," he murmurs into my hair before planting a kiss on the top of my head. It's the reminder I need.

"When I came home from school on the thirteenth, my mom told me what the teacher asked her to do. Surprisingly, she had already gone out and bought two dozen red-frosted cupcakes from the convenience store.

When she showed them to me, she told me I better enjoy them, because that was the last thing she was buying for me until her EBT card reloaded the next month."

I can still smell the stench of stale smoke that clung to our trailer like a cancer. I can see my mother sitting at her perch in the front room, carelessly flicking ash all over the couch that doubled as my bed.

Bile rises up my esophagus, threatening to spill over.

"Jo."

My eyes find Kylian's. His steady gaze snaps me back to reality.

I am here. This is now.

I'll never be in a situation like that again. I'll make sure of it. They'll make sure of it. But that doesn't mean all the grief I feel for the little girl who had to be so strong and callous just to survive isn't valid.

When Kylian's icy blue irises stay fixed on mine—holding me steady, reminding and assuring me I'm safe—I finally break. The tears I've been trying to hold back burst through me like a geyser.

He sidles up to my free side, pressing me into Nicky and soothingly stroking my hair. I let myself feel it, I let myself be soft and vulnerable, because I know between the four of them, they can handle it.

I sob for what feels like hours, though I suspect only a few minutes have actually passed. When I finally settle, I wipe my snotty nose on Nicky's hoodie sleeves and take the deepest breath I've taken all day.

"Our Valentine's Day class party was on a Thursday, right before a long weekend. There were twenty-two kids in my class including me, plus the teacher. I brought home one cupcake, and that plus whatever was still edible in the fridge in our trailer was all I had to eat until classes resumed four days later. I didn't see my mom at all that weekend. I don't think I ever saw her on any of my birthdays again."

I sniffle, more angry than sad when I let the reality of her choices sink in. I wipe a stray tear from my face, upset with myself that I fell about just now.

That's the thing about trauma—I never know how it's going to rear its head, just that it's not going to feel good when it happens.

"I understand my reaction earlier upset you." My focus shifts to my husband; I know him well enough to know he took my rejection the hardest. "But I hate this day. It's always been marked with fear or disappointment. I hate those memories, and I hate the reminder of how helpless I was back then."

"You were a child," Decker seethes.

I shrug out of Nicky's and Kylian's embraces to close the space between us.

"I know," I assure my husband as I wrap my arms around his torso and rest my chin on his sternum.

His arms find their rightful place around my waist. His hands splay wide on my low back, pinning my body to his.

"I can't just flip a switch and change how I feel, though, Cap. I don't want to have to fake it with you," I tell him sincerely. "With any of you," I add, looking to each of my guys. "I don't like my birthday for very valid reasons. I might grow to like it eventually... but I can't promise that. I think it's going to take years of low-key, non-drama February fourteenths for me to truly embrace this day."

They're all quiet, which gives me hope I got through.

"Thank you for sharing that with us," Kendrick tells me, holding out his hand.

I willingly take it, but Decker doesn't release me right away. Instead, he kisses my forehead and gives me a sorrowful frown, though he does then reluctantly let me go.

When I step into Kendrick's embrace, another wave of security washes over me.

I am here. This is now. And this is a very good place to be.

"I still want to celebrate Valentine's Day with you," I tell them, resting my cheek against K's chest. "This weekend was off to an amazing start, and I'm so happy to be here. I just don't want to make it about my birthday, if that's okay."

"Of course it's okay," Kylian replies. He looks to the others but doesn't give them time to object. "What do you need right now, baby?"

I press my lips together, thinking. "The balloons and decorations are gone?"

"Every single one," he confirms.

Decker adds, "I can take out the trash so you don't see them again. I'll wipe down all the counters. Clear out all the evidence."

I silently laugh against K's chest. My husband is a stubborn, obstinate man. But once he finally gets it, he really fucking gets it.

A yawn catches me by surprise.

"How about a bath, Mama?" Kendrick offers. "That way you can relax while Cap does a thorough sweep of the scene of the crime."

I have to fight back another laugh. "That sounds like heaven."

Chapter 13

Locke

I catch Joey's wrist when she turns to follow the others inside. "Hey. Not so fast."

Brows scrunched, she stops and looks back to me. "What's up?"

I can't stand the space between us. I take both her hands in mine and step as close as physically possible. Then I place a tender kiss on her lips. "I'm sorry," I whisper.

"Nicky..."

I silence her with another kiss. This one feels more urgent, my soul desperate to atone for everything that just went down. I pour my apology into the kiss, caressing my tongue against hers in a solemn prayer the begs for forgiveness.

When I finally pull away, she's breathless. Good. Now maybe I can get this out.

"The others only knew about your birthday because of me," I confess. "I saw it marked on Kylian's calendar two days ago, then I went ahead and told Kendrick and Cap so we could try and salvage the weekend. But all I did was ruin things."

Her fingers brush through the hair at my nape. "This isn't your fault, Emo Boy. You're not responsible for their behavior. If anything, I should be apologizing to you."

"What? Why?"

"It's not like I was going to be able to keep my birthday a secret forever. I should have known someone would figure it out, and I should have been proactive about the fact that I did not want to celebrate or even acknowledge the day."

Sighing, I bury my face in her hair. "I guess we all could have done things differently."

Joey scoffs, her shoulders shaking. "You can say that again. But things like this are going to happen. We're still figuring this relationship out, but we're all doing our best. My knee-jerk reaction isn't anyone's fault. I hate that I reacted the way I did. Thank you for loving me, even when I'm not that easy to love."

"Always, Hot Girl. And you are easy to love. I might not get it right, but I swear I'll always try."

"I think that's the secret. As long as we keep learning and stay committed to loving each other in the ways we want and need to be loved, we'll all be okay in the end."

"I love you," I tell her, the words rolling off my tongue with such ease it takes my breath away. "And even if it's not my fault, I am still sorry I caused you pain."

"I'll always love you, Nicky."

And that right there is all I need to know. I might not always get it right. I'm bound to mess up when it comes to my girl. But I'll never stop trying, and I'll never tire of finding new ways to show her how much she means to me. Which reminds me...

"The birthday presents were a hard no, and I completely understand why." I crane back so I can see her reaction to what I say next. "But what if someone had a Valentine's Day gift they really wanted to give you?"

With one eyebrow cocked, she hits me with an unamused look. "What is it?"

Well, shit. Now I really wish I would have just taken my shirt off last night.

"Let's start with what it isn't," I hedge.

She's already wearing my hoodie. That means there's only a thin cotton T-shirt hiding my big reveal.

"It isn't something tangible, and it's not something that can be wrapped."

Her pretty blue eyes narrow. I can see the wheels turning as she tries to figure it out.

"Is it expensive?"

I grimace. I won't lie to her. "Technically, yes. But it's the kind of thing I would have spent money on regardless of whether it was for you."

Joey scrunches her nose, clearly still unsure.

I decide to change my approach. "How about this? Your birthday doesn't mean shit to me, Hot Girl."

Joey cackles, and a wave of relief crashes over me.

"But you? You're my entire world. So for Valentine's Day, I wanted to do something to honor you and to show you just how deeply I love the woman you are."

I whip my shirt off, then proudly turn around and give her my back. When her little gasp reaches my ears, I can't stand to not see her face. I look over my shoulder, eager to witness her reaction.

With both hands pressed to her mouth, she stares, wide-eyed.

"Is that..."

The words are drenched in emotion. I feel a tightness in my chest as I watch the realization of what I've done sink in.

"I gave you my jersey and my number. I know, legally, you took Decker's last name. But I wanted to do something special to make sure you knew that you own me, Hot Girl. Body, mind, and soul."

"Can I touch it?" she whispers.

I grin, then nod. "No nails, though. I just had the final session last week, so it's still healing and itchy as hell in a few spots."

The heat of her breath tickles my skin. One fingertip traces the nine letters of her name, which are nearly ten inches tall and span my entire upper back.

J-O-S-E-P-H-I-N-E

When she reaches the bottom of the last E, I turn around and kiss her fiercely. She returns the kiss with just as much intensity. It's only the frigid air chilling my skin that prevents me from deepening the kiss and seeing where this goes, right now, out here on the deck.

Begrudgingly, I pull back. But I keep her wrapped up in my arms as I share my truth. "I love you, Josephine. You're permanently etched into my skin and forever imprinted in my soul."

"Loving you is easier than breathing, Nicky." She cranes back, teary-eyed, and presses her forehead into mine. "Thank you for seeing me and for loving me so well."

Chapter 14
Kendrick

"Come on, Mama. You're wrinkled like a prune."

I secure the towel around my waist, then offer Jojo my hand.

She slowly rises out of the water, a fucking vision all wet and pliable from our soak. I scan her luscious curves as water sluices down her torso and legs. Is it strange to admit I'm jealous of water? Nah. I'm obsessed with this woman. There's no shame in the way I crave her.

She uses my hand for balance as she steps over the ledge and out of the tub. "Should I be concerned that we just took a bath and you didn't even attempt to fuck me?"

Goddamn. The sass from this girl.

Although I guess it's a fair question. I can't recall the last time I had her in the shower... in the bath... or hell, even in the hot tub back at the isle, and it didn't lead to more. Fucking her wet is one of my favorite ways to have her.

When I'm sure she's steady on her feet, I grip her chin and tip her head back to meet my gaze. "You know getting dirty with you then cleaning you up is my favorite, Mama. But this afternoon wasn't about me. It was about you. To take your mind off things. To help you relax. Because it's *Valentine's Day*," I quickly clarify before capturing her mouth in a hard kiss. "And because nothing satisfies me more than taking care of my woman."

She doesn't argue as I wrap a fresh towel around her body and secure it. What she does do is hit me with those gorgeous bright blue bedroom eyes framed by thick lashes. Ignoring her wanton stare, I guide her toward the vanity and grab another clean towel off the stack. Blotting the wet ends of her hair, I catch her heated gaze in the mirror.

"Don't look at me like that, Mama," I warn. Kyl's been texting me for thirty minutes about dinner, trying to hurry us along. "The boys are waiting on us."

She bites down on her plush lower lip, her eyes never leaving mine.

Chuckling to myself, I reach across the sink and grab a brush and a hair elastic, then get to work brushing out her hair.

"One or two?" I ask, holding up the single elastic.

"One is good," she replies.

I make quick work of twisting her hair into a thick braid. When I'm done, I move the plait to one side, smooth my hands over her bare shoulders, and place a kiss at the top of her spine.

The bath clearly helped soothe her nerves. I think she'll be thrilled with what we have planned for the rest of the night, too.

With that in mind, I shoot my shot and broach the topic I've been itching to talk about all afternoon.

After placing a soft kiss on her bare shoulder, I say, "About the necklace..."

Jojo turns around and faces me, her expression still cool and even.

"I'm sorry for the way I reacted, K. But it still feels like too much."

That's what I was afraid of. But I'm not giving up that easily.

"Too much how?"

She averts her gaze, a clear sign that she's uncomfortable. I don't want to make her upset, and I don't want her to shut down on me again, but I need to understand, and I hope like hell that there's enough love and trust between us to encourage her to hear me out and try to understand where I'm coming from, too.

I cup her cheek in one hand, tilting her face back toward me. "Talk to me, Mama," I coax.

With a slow swallow, she nods. Her voice is uncharacteristically soft when she speaks. "The necklace was beautiful. But it looked really expensive."

It kills me to know she doesn't think she's worthy of this type of gift. But the necklace was never supposed to be about her birthday. Hell, I didn't even plan to give it to her for Valentine's Day—the timing just worked out like that.

"It was expensive," I confirm. I won't lie to her. "But it's also more than just a necklace."

Her eyes flit up and meet my gaze in the mirror.

"Can I show it to you again?"

She presses her lips together, and I wait her out. If she says no, I'll respect that boundary. But I hope like hell she'll hear me out.

"Okay," she finally agrees.

I bend down and pull the jewelry box out of my discarded pants. When I right myself, I hold out the box and open it slowly, bringing my lips to her ear to explain.

"The green gemstones are emeralds. They used to be my Ma's."

Her sharp intake of breath confirms I've got her attention now.

"She left them to me and told me I'd know what to do with them when I met the right person." I place another wet, lingering kiss on top of my girl's shoulder.

"The diamonds between the emeralds? I bought those myself."

She shivers. "So those are real diamonds?"

I keep my mouth on her skin but lift my gaze to find her worried expression in the mirror. "They are," I murmur, trailing more kisses along her neck.

"Ever since I started getting NIL deals, every dollar I've earned went back to my Pops for the girls. That was my choice. I want them to go to the best schools and to never have to worry about anything. But then last weekend happened."

Joey's eyebrows shoot up in question.

"Knowing how well things went at the Combine made it all feel real for me. Having you by my side, knowing this dream is actually about to come true? I wanted to celebrate. For the first time in my life, I wanted to use my hard-earned money on something I wanted: a gift for the person I love most."

"Kendrick."

My name is soft and breathy coming out of her pretty little mouth.

"I want to spend the rest of my life spoiling you, Jojo. Worshipping you. Letting the whole damn world know that you are it for me."

She leans back against my chest, then lifts one hand to her throat.

"Will you put it on me?"

I grin. I can't fucking help it. "With pleasure," I tell her, stringing the tennis-style necklace around her delicate neck and clasping it right where it belongs.

Gripping her hips, I bend low and bring my mouth to her ear once more. I don't miss the way she rolls her ass back into my body. Arousal shoots through me, feeling her bare skin against mine in the reflection of the mirror.

"Can I tell you my favorite part about this necklace?"

She hums contently.

I loosen the towel wrapped around her body, letting it fall to the floor. Starting low, I run my palm up the length of her spine, applying more pressure the higher I climb.

She whimpers when I cuff the back of her neck, and when I trace one finger around the closure of the jewelry, she sinks back into my hold.

"I made sure there were diamonds on the whole length of the chain. That way, everyone knows you're mine, but then I also get to see them shine when I fuck you from behind."

Her breath hitches, and she reaches back for me, clumsily pulling at the towel around my waist.

"How we feelin' about this necklace now, Mama?"

"K," she whines.

"Nuh-uh. I need your words."

She emits a growl of frustration, whips around to face me, and yanks my towel free. "I love the necklace. Happy? Now fuck me," she demands.

I nip at her lips and shake my head. When I pull back, my mind glitches at the sight before me. She's completely naked and fresh-faced, wearing nothing but the jewelry I gave her.

"Where are your manners?"

She huffs again. I fight back a laugh.

"Please, Kendrick. Please fuck me," she begs. Her nails scrape up the length of my chest.

I hiss, reveling in the pain that morphs into the promise of pleasure. "Turn around and grip the counter, Mama."

She complies and meets my gaze in the mirror once more.

"Your eyes don't leave that mirror while I'm fucking you. Understood?"

"Fuck. Yes." She pushes her ass back into my cock, taunting me.

I brush her clit with my fingers, but quickly travel up the length of her torso, over her chest, and bring my hand all the way to her face.

"Mouth."

She opens for me.

"Relax," I command, dipping two fingers between her lips and pressing down on her tongue. Her mouth fills with saliva as her tongue laps around the intrusion.

Once my fingers are nice and wet, I bring them down between her legs.

"Wider," I instruct.

She gasps when I shove two fingers into her cunt. She spasms on contact, my perfect, responsive girl.

"Fucking love to feel you clench around me like that," I groan. I rest my forehead against her back, then trail little kisses along her shoulder as my fingers work her into a frenzy.

When I look at her reflection to see just how pretty the crystalline and green jewels look against her flushed skin, she's got her eyes closed and her head tipped back in ecstasy.

"Nuh-uh," I scold, withdrawing my hand from her pussy.

Her eyes shoot open just like I knew they would. Her lips part as she prepares to sass me, but I stick the two fingers covered in her juices right back into her mouth to silence her.

"If you want my cock, you'll keep your eyes on the mirror, just like I fucking told you."

Groaning, she sucks on my fingers and nods.

I keep them pressed firmly against her tongue, line my cock up, and push in with one good thrust.

Her whole body jolts, her throat and her cunt pulsating in tandem as she fucking takes it.

Warmth and wetness surround me, her tight little pussy choking on my cock as I bend my knees and bury myself to the hilt, then press her harder into the counter.

I focus on her perfect ass, fixating on the way her cheeks flex for me every time I press into her. Keeping a steady rhythm, I drink her in, and I groan when my gaze lands on the jewels she let me place around her neck.

My woman. My life force. My pride and fucking joy.

When I glance back to the mirror, she's watching me intently, just like she promised.

"That's it, Mama. Fucking take it. And keep those eyes on me."

She whimpers when I pull my fingers out of her mouth. I position that hand between her pelvis and the countertop, making sure I'm perfectly lined up so her clit hits my palm with every thrust.

"K," she pants, her breathing coming in short, fast huffs. "Fuck. Fuck me *harder*."

As if she even has to ask.

I drill into her, pounding her body into the sink, taking care to cushion her sweet spot as I drive us both higher and higher.

"You were made for this, Mama. Made to take me. Made to be loved in every fucking way I plan to love you."

I'm close, but I hold back.

I feel it building, that telltale tingle, but I won't fucking come until she's blissed out and over the edge.

My fingertips find her clit, pinching it and applying even more pressure.

I pound into her so hard my thighs burn. I drive forward with so much momentum the vanity creaks from our weight.

Between thrusts, I bear my fucking soul, begging this woman to let me love her and show her how vital she is to me and to our family.

"Let me—"

Thrust.

"—fucking—"

Thrust.

"—love you."

Thrust.

She detonates, screaming and pushing back on my cock, always trying to give as good as she gets.

Deep, rapid spasms of her perfect pussy pull my own orgasm right out of me. My hot cum fills her cunt, both of us left panting and breathless.

I pull out quickly, cup one hand between her thighs, and gather up as much of my release as I can.

"K, what—"

"One more," I demand. With one finger over her clit and two in her cunt, I work my well-coated thumb into her tight little asshole. "Let me play with these pretty little holes and make you come again, Mama."

"Fuck," she whimpers, overwhelmed by the intrusion.

Her body's still coming down from the first wave, and already, she's clenching all around me.

"K, I can't. I can't just—"

I crook two fingers along her G-spot and work her clit hard and fast. "You can and you will. Give me one more, Mama. Show me how much you love being my girl."

Determination sweeps over her features. She presses back, rolls her hips, and fucks herself on my hand as I bring her right back to the brink.

With my eyes locked with hers, I mouth, "I love you."

Once more, she fucking explodes around me.

Her tight holes suck me in, pulsating around my hand. Her release and my cum drip all over, making a fucking mess down her inner thighs.

She's right there—surrounding me, completing me.

In this moment, lids heavy, expression sated, and my jewelry around her neck, she's never looked more beautiful. Or more like *mine*.

Chapter 15

Joey

I needed a shower after K fucked me from behind in front of the mirror. We both did, actually, but he rinsed quickly and told me to take my time and join them when I was ready. Apparently, Kylian had been pestering him about our whereabouts, but he promised to run interference.

I scrubbed my skin clean and reveled in the post-orgasm bliss for several minutes. Although I recognize it's not just the orgasms I'm blissed out from right now.

Kendrick took such tender, loving care of me all afternoon. His explanation about the necklace and what it means to him helped me tremendously. It was also the reminder I needed.

Even if I react poorly or am having a hard time, I owe it to my guys to hear them out. Relationships are two-way streets. Or in our case, more like a five-lane highway. I need to try my best to communicate my needs while also staying open as we learn and grow together.

After my shower, I throw on clean sweats and a tank top, then secure my necklace from K in its rightful place. By the time I make my way into the kitchen, I'm feeling so much more settled about this day.

As I turn the corner, I see all four of my guys hovering around the kitchen island, talking among themselves. I pause, letting my gaze drift from man to man.

Contentment washes over me. How lucky am I to be loved by all of them?

As I pad across the floor, Decker spots me first. His dark obsidian eyes bore into my soul, regret and concern radiating from him as I approach.

I go directly to his side, wrap my arms around his waist, and press up on tiptoes. "We're okay, Cap," I assure him. Just in case that's what he needs to hear. Then I kiss him sweetly, letting my hands travel up his broad back until my fingers are tangled in his hair.

Kylian clears his throat.

I break away from my husband, grinning. "Yes, Daddy?"

He stares at me, deadpan, through his glasses. "Come here."

I give Decker one last peck, then dash into Kylian's arms.

"You're okay."

It's a statement, an assessment, and a question, all concealed in two little words.

"I'm okay." I hug him close and let him hold me. I hate that my reaction today affected him. Especially because I suspect Kylian did not contribute to any of the birthday overwhelm, despite being the original source of information.

He brushes my braid out of the way and brings his lips to my ear. "Today has been weird. Tomorrow is Sunday. You'll be down in the Den by seven a.m. and not a minute later."

Okay then. That's a full two hours earlier than our usual Sunday morning routine. Clearly, Daddy wants to play.

I get it. I hate feeling off with any of my guys.

I nod my assent, then rest my cheek against his shirt. Scanning the kitchen once more, I note all the takeout containers and pizza boxes spread across the countertops.

"What's all this?" I ask, looking from the island to the table.

"Oh, this?" Nicky asks nonchalantly. "This is just a cozy night at the cabin. Dinner, drinks, poker." He wags his eyebrows at me. Knowing my guys, there's a very particular type of poker we'll be playing tonight.

Nicky continues. "You'll notice we ordered pizza *and* Chinese food—not because it's a special occasion, but because we didn't know what you'd be in the mood for. We're using paper plates, and we didn't even bother setting out napkins. Grab a paper towel if you need it."

I roll my eyes at his ridiculousness. Kylian swats my ass when he notices.

"This is just a cozy night in, the five of us together. Is that okay with you?"

My smile takes over my entire face as I nod. I'm so damn lucky to be loved by them.

Kendrick moves around the island, grabbing a few bottles, then nodding toward me. "I'm making drinks. What'll it be, Mama?"

I hold his gaze for a moment, a shuddering breath rolling through me when his focus lowers to the necklace and his eyes heat with satisfaction.

"I'll have a Tom Collins." As if that's a surprise to anyone.

With a silent squeeze, I release Kylian, then make my way over to Nicky.

He cradles me against his chest, my back to his front, wrapping his enormous tatted arms around me and holding me with loving care.

Craning back, I say, "This is perfect. Thank you."

He bends low, nuzzling into my neck, then giving me a playful nip. "I didn't have the heart to get rid of the cake. It's out on the deck. We can ignore it completely, but—"

My lips meet his, effectively cutting him off with a kiss. When we break apart, I offer him a reassuring smile.

"It would be a shame to let good cake go to waste."

Nicky grins right back at me. "My thoughts exactly."

Chapter 16

Joey

The blue light from a screen casts a soft glow around the usually dark room as I slip inside and close the door.

The low-light digital clock switches from 6:59 to 7:00 a.m. Right on time.

"Get on the bed."

Without hesitation, I pull my shirt over my head and step out of my sleep shorts and panties as I approach. Kyl and I have this routine down to a science. I know what he wants—how he expects me to present myself. Just like I know that he's going to give me a high like no other, and all I have to do is submit.

I also know what following this routine does for him. Hell, what it does for me, too. He's not the only one who needs this one-on-one time. I crave the consistency of Sunday mornings the way my lungs crave my next breath.

I crawl up the mattress and drape my limbs across his body as he sets his phone on the nightstand and wraps his arms around my bare back.

Kylian's steady heartbeat reverberates through me. Sinking into him, I slow my breathing to match his pace. His hands go wide on my low back, gripping me with a reciprocated sense of need.

My body calms. My heart settles. My entire sense of self renews as we slot into place.

"Good morning," I eventually murmur, lifting my head to place a kiss in the center of his chest. Kyl may not be as big as my other guys, but the muscle he does have is hard and defined.

"Are you okay?" he probes.

I let the question wash over me. There's not a right answer. If I wasn't okay, he would honor that, and our Sunday morning would look very different.

But that's the beauty of truly being seen and being loved so well.

Yesterday I started to spiral.

But I was able to stop, regroup, and open up about what was bothering me instead of letting it fester or grow into a monster I was scared to confront.

It's okay to not be okay. That doesn't make me a burden or difficult to love. It's part of being human. It's part of surviving something awful and then refusing to let it corrupt the best parts of life.

I give him a confident nod. "Yes. I'm okay."

He watches me, his bright blue eyes barely visible through the lenses of his glasses. After a few beats, he nods once, accepting my answer.

I roll my lips together as he stares at me.

"What is it, baby?"

Warmth radiates through my chest. Kyl can always tell when there's something on my mind.

"You didn't get me anything," I state. I'm not upset by the lack of gifts—on the contrary, I love that he read between the lines and correctly assessed the context of the situation.

He hooks his hands under the meaty part of my ass and shifts me higher up his body. I pop up on my elbows, wanting to see as much of him as I can despite the darkness.

"I assumed you would react poorly to the receiving of unrequested, unexpected gifts."

That tracks. Kylian explained at Christmas how stressful it felt to not know what he was receiving as a kid. He asked each of us for a specific gift and even sent the order link to ensure we purchased the right version of what he requested. None of the guys balked, and once he explained how uncomfortable he was with the uncertainty of surprise gift-giving, I quickly came to terms with it, too.

His inclination to avoid surprising me makes sense.

I bite down on my bottom lip, silently debating whether I want to ask the other question that's been nagging at me since yesterday. I clear my throat and find my courage. "You didn't think to warn the others?"

Kylian sighs. "I tried. In retrospect, I should have tried much harder. I realize that now," he confesses. "I did not have the bandwidth to talk Decker and Kendrick out of their grandiose ideas. I just wanted to get away from the mansion and enjoy this weekend together. I've been overextending myself, trying to help Spence and keep up with the security detail for Hunter. I thought I was coping well, but there are a lot of people at the house right now, and obviously, I'm slipping."

"Kylian. No. I didn't mean—"

"I recognize the role I should have played in this situation, Jo. I'm not accepting all the blame or berating myself, but I know I could have done better. Could have, should have, and decidedly will moving forward."

We're both quiet as I let his words soothe me. I'm glad I asked, because now I have a better idea of everything he's dealing with, too. Eventually, I lift my head and peak up at him once more.

"So... besides the sprinkles, which I really did love, by the way..." He smiles, and my insides tingle. "There aren't any more surprises?"

We're leaving around lunchtime. I would be shocked if there was anything else, but my anxiety still needs to know for sure.

"I'm making pancakes for breakfast after I eat you out for several hours. That's the last surprise I planned for this weekend."

Contentment washes over me.

"I can live with pancakes."

Kylian snickers.

"No comment on the other part of the morning that's about to commence?"

I rest my chin on his chest, willing him to feel my sincerity. "No comment, but only because my feelings are a given. Sunday mornings are my favorite part of every week."

With a salacious grin, he says, "Don't get ahead of yourself, baby. You haven't tried these pancakes yet."

I snort-laugh, my chest bouncing with amusement as I try to keep it together. Kylian never used to joke. I love when he makes wise-cracks or offers up a quippy remark.

Black and white. Cut and dry. I love life with this man. I love the structure and security he provides. Right now, and for every day after this, I know how lucky I am to be loved by Kylian Walsh.

His body tenses below me, and his brows knit together. "Wait. I just thought of something else."

"What?" I demand, slightly panicked.

Flipping us, he frames my head with his forearms and hovers just out of reach. "There's a high probability you're going to be thanking me for what I'm about to give you. I've gathered enough anecdotal evidence to reason you may even beg for more. Following that strain of logic, one could assume that my tongue, my mouth, and my cock are all presents."

This time, I snort. "You're so full of it."

I settle on my back, getting into position, and spread my legs wide, then press my hands into the headboard. I know the drill. I know how he wants to take me. I'll do anything for this man. Submitting to his hyperfixation on my pussy truly is what I love most about Sundays.

"I think what you meant is 'May I have my gift now, Daddy?'"

I bite down on my bottom lip, eyeing him lasciviously as he holds himself in plank position and rakes his gaze along my body.

"I want everything you have to give me, Daddy."

His gaze heats with desire. "Say it again."

"Please, Daddy?" I ask sweetly. "Please can I have my gift?"

He adjusts his glasses, places both his hands on my inner thighs, and spreads me open wider, licking his lips before he lowers himself and brings his mouth to my core.

Chapter 17
Kylian

The intersection of art and science must converge in synchronicity to create a perfect pancake.

Despite being deceptively simple in presentation, precise measurements, consistent heat, and proper execution are all required to accomplish excellence.

I've always prescribed to the notion that if something is worth doing, it's worth doing well.

Which is why I spent three separate mornings at my parents' house last month, observing everything I could from my dad's pancake-making lessons. I then practiced my technique on six occasions leading up to this weekend.

Spence has just about had it with the carb loading I've required of him during our late-night planning sessions.

I smirk and consider texting Kabir a picture to prove that all my preparation was not in vain. The batch I'm flipping now is fluffy, crisp around the edges, and consistently shaped. In a single word: perfection.

Kendrick saunters over, shirtless, with a coffee mug in hand. He keeps his distance, respecting my space. I have absolutely no problem rubbing bodies when we're in the heat of the moment pleasing our woman. Any other time, I prefer a hands-off approach with anyone but Jo.

"Need any help, Daddy Genius?"

I keep my focus set on the pancakes, especially the one in the middle of the pan. The make and model of this range is identical to the one I practiced on at home, but we're on propane out here. The slightest variation could disrupt the final product. I didn't come this far to only come this far.

"I've got one more batch to cook after this. Can you see if Jo's awake?"

He takes off toward the Den—it is Sunday, after all—and I keep watching those edges, biding my time as I wait for the ideal moment to flip.

I'm arranging the final batch of pancakes on a serving plate when everyone starts to trickle into the kitchen.

"Good morning," Jo singsongs as she makes the rounds, greeting the others. Her hair is wet, so she must have showered. I hope she rested, too. Four orgasms isn't a record for us, but after the weekend she's endured—and with what Decker has planned tonight—I need to stay cognizant of her baser needs.

She wraps her arms around me last. Wordlessly, I reach over and snag a water bottle I already prepared for her. I can practically feel her eye roll as I bring the straw to her lips. She takes a long draw, then takes the bottle from my hands.

"Good girl," I murmur, adding the last pancake to the stack.

When I allow myself to glance over at her, she's eyeing the plate of pancakes in my hand with intense interest.

"Those smell amazing," she practically moans.

My chest inflates with pride. "I would hope so. I used my dad's recipe. I spent seventeen hours practicing and perfecting my technique. I even brought the correct maple syrup to go with them."

Locke scoffs from the table. "The *correct* maple syrup?"

I shoot him an incredulous look. "Yes. Real maple syrup, sourced from a small-batch family-owned business located in the Maple Belt of Quebec. Do you have any idea what they put in American table syrups?" I shudder at the thought.

"I have a feeling we're about to find out," Kendrick grumbles, reaching over and loading his plate with several pancakes from the stack.

I snag a few of the warmest ones for Jo, quickly adding a pad of butter between the short stack so it can properly melt.

"Dude. You sound pretentious as hell." Locke laughs. He stabs his fork into the pile to transfer them to his plate. "What's next? Are you going to tell us it's only real maple syrup if it comes from the 'Maple Belt' of Canada?"

Everyone laughs, but the joke's on them if they prefer to ingest corn syrup, caramel color, and diglycerides.

"Wait. Shit. This is the Brit's influence, isn't it?"

I side-eye Nicky, considering his assumption about Spence. Jo's warned me that my recent 'bromance' (her word, not mine) might make my best friend jealous. Because of that, I refrain from replying.

I admire Spence, and our recently established joint ventures will prove advantageous to me for years to come.

But nothing and no one can change how I feel for the very first person who ever saw me for me. Nicky is my brother in every way that matters. Not even Jo can dislodge the love I have for my oldest friend.

"Fine," I declare flippantly. "I won't offer you any of the correct maple syrup. The one with the red cap is the table syrup. Help yourself."

Kendrick points his fork at Nicky, then says through a mouthful, "You better try these for yourself before you keep running your mouth and he takes away all your pancake privileges. These are fucking delicious."

With a satisfied smirk, I take a bite.

Perfection.

Pride washes over me.

Only the best for this family.

Decker finally takes a seat, pulling Jo into his arms and positioning her in his lap. I let them have their moment but take care to cut a small triangle from Jo's stack and bring it to her mouth.

"Open, baby."

She obeys, clamping down on the fork harder than necessary.

But then she closes her eyes and emits a satisfied moan.

"Oh my god. Are you kidding me? Try these!" she tells Decker, digging into her stack with the side of her fork and offering him his first taste.

I lean back in my chair, equally pleased and gratified by her reaction. "You like that, baby?"

"Like? Try love. Or hell, in the words of Hunter, I *flove* them. We might need to add this into the permanent rotation on Sundays," she teases. "'Daddy's Special Recipe' has a nice ring to it, dontcha think?"

Chapter 18

Decker

One by one, we file out the front door of the cabin with bags, dirty laundry, and leftover food in tow.

Josephine is the last one out, trailing behind me, but I block her in as soon as she steps over the threshold.

Framing the door with one arm, I fix my gaze on the love of my life. "I'm driving home. Will you sit up front with me?"

She gives me a beaming smile. "Of course." Popping up on her tiptoes, she wraps one arm around my neck and gives me the sweetest, most tender kiss.

Someone honks the horn, trying to hurry us along.

I keep kissing her, refusing to pull away until I'm good and ready, offering my middle finger in the general direction of the others.

They're clued in and on board—literally—with what I'm planning to do when we get back to the marina. I should be thankful all they're doing is honking the damn car horn. I wouldn't put it past any of them to tease me about stalling or to start up with the boat jokes.

"I love you, Decker," Josephine whispers against my lips before finally pulling away. "Promise me we can come back up here and skate again before it gets too warm? Even if it's just for the day. Just you and me?"

My ego preens. "Of course, Siren."

There isn't anything I wouldn't do for her. There isn't anything I can refuse her. She's given me everything, just by being who she is. I want to spend my entire life showing her how grateful I am for her love.

I lock up, then wrap my arm around her as we walk to the truck.

I open the passenger door and help her climb in, then double-check her seat belt. That earns me an eye roll, but I don't care.

Nothing is more precious to me.

Rounding the car, I find the others waiting at the trunk.

"All set?" I ask, loading my bag as well as Josephine's, then pulling closed the hatch.

"Everything's been arranged to your specifications," Kylian confirms.

Kendrick rubs his hands together, a devilish smile painted across his face. "We're really doing this, Cap?"

Locke scoffs. "He better be *really doing this*. Otherwise it's going to be a long-ass night of him watching us fuck our girl in the middle of the lake."

The tic in my jaw is the reminder I need.

Unclench. Breathe. Remember what and who it's all for.

"We're doing this," I declare. No turning back now. I called the play. With a deep, grounding inhale, I smack the side of the truck two times. "Load up. Let's go."

I give myself one minute to worry about how tonight will go down. The idea was simple enough. When I explained it to the others, they assured me Josephine would love it. That was enough to build up my confidence that this is what I want to do.

I always have had to learn my lesson the hardest way possible when it comes to my wife. But I always fucking learn. I'll never stop trying to please her.

She loved ice-skating. Hell, she loved all the surprises we planned for her this weekend, save for the over-the-top gifts and the unexpected birthday stuff.

When it comes to Josephine, I tend to get it wrong before I get it right.

But I'll never stop trying, which means I can't fail.

I open the truck door and look over to where she sits. Her soft smile greets me, and the sincerity in her gaze galvanizes me.

Once I'm seated behind the wheel, she reaches over and squeezes my thigh. I catch her hand in mine, bring it to my mouth, and kiss her knuckles.

"Let's go home," she tells me.

I don't need to put the car in drive or even move a muscle to fulfill her request. Home is wherever she is, and wherever we can all be together.

Chapter 19

Josephine

"What is all this?"

I'm staring at a boat—one of ours, I think—but it's practically unrecognizable under the mountains of jewel-toned pillows and blankets piled on every surface. The tables and chairs usually set up in the middle have been cleared. Every inch of the vessel has been transformed into a love nest.

"Pretty sure this is your wildest fantasy come to life," Kylian quips.

I whip my head around and search his face. He cocks one eyebrow, then shifts his gaze to Decker.

"Are you serious right now?" Laughing, I turn to my husband. This whole setup can't really mean what I think it means.

Decker has rules. Decker *loves* his stupid rules. Boat sex has always been a no-no (with the exception of one fantastic night where Kylian led me from guy to guy by my ponytail so I could suck them off).

My husband scowls at my apparent disbelief.

The other three? They look like they're trying their hardest not to absolutely lose it.

I press my lips together and lift my hand to my mouth. I have to calm down. I can't laugh. If Decker's really going to go for this, I don't want to spook him.

When I meet his hard gaze, all amusement evaporates like it's been excised from my soul. His piercing glare is so hot, so irritated and intense, I shiver.

"Get on the boat before I change my mind, Josephine."

That shuts me up real quick.

I climb aboard, not sure where to even step with the soft blankets covering every surface. Should I take my shoes off? What are the rules for Decker's floating love nest?

A hard body sidles up behind me, the frame eclipsing mine and sending a jolt of anticipation from the top of my head to the tips of my toes. Warm breath tickles my neck when the man behind me brings his lips to my ear.

"Strip and lie down, Mrs. Crusade. Let's see if the reality of what I have planned for you lives up to your wildest fantasy."

I'm surrounded. Overwhelmed. Overstimulated. *Obsessed*.

I'm lying—bare—in the middle of the pontoon, which has been anchored in the center of the lake.

The blankets beneath me are heated, their warmth combined with the heat radiating off my guys' bodies providing all the climate control I need.

They're touching me everywhere: their hands caressing my skin, their lips exploring every crevice. I feel warm all over, so wonderfully wanted, as they worship every inch of skin they can find.

Decker captures my mouth, feeding me his tongue as he grinds his erection into my core, hovering over my body to give the others easier access.

Kylian teases one nipple between his teeth as his fingertips trail up and down the hollow of my throat.

Nicky and K must have planned ahead, because they're basically mirroring each other's movements but on opposite sides of my body. Each man nips at one of my inner thighs, alternating turns as they torturously drag their tongues toward my center, then pulls back without actually touching me where I crave them most.

Panting, Decker breaks away from my mouth, resting his forehead on mine. "I could spend the rest of my life kissing you, Siren, and it still wouldn't be enough."

My fingers scrape through the short hairs at his nape. I try to pull his lips back to mine, but he resists.

"What do you want?" he asks, his voice husky as his obsidian eyes search my face.

Kylian clamps down on my nipple and sucks hard. I arch my back instinctively when he releases me, practically floating as my torso brushes against Decker's defined chest.

I'm breathless. Weightless. Drifting wherever the boat takes us. Succumbing to whatever pleasure my boys dole out.

Refocusing on my husband, I nip at his lips. "I want you to make me come," I plead. Every inch of my skin is on fire. I'm so needy my cunt feels like it has its own heartbeat.

Gulping, Decker nods once. "Who do you want to make you come, Siren?"

Realization flashes through me like lightning.

Gripping the back of his head with both hands, I look my husband in the eye. "You, Decker. I need *you* to make me come."

His lashes flutter closed. His chest shudders above me.

When he opens his eyes, heat blazes behind impossibly dark irises.

My words were clearly both a comfort and a confidence boost.

Decker pulls back, then drags his hand between my breasts as he works his way down... down... down.

With a roguish smile and hooded eyes, he scans my naked, writhing frame. "Your wish is my command, wife."

He wraps his arms around my legs, lifting my lower half off the floor of the boat. "Hold her open for me," he tells Kendrick and Locke. They each take a leg, supporting my weight as my husband situates himself at my core.

Decker doesn't ease me into it. He doesn't tease or gently caress to build up the tension. He dives in, devouring my sex and sucking so hard on my clit I see stars.

My back tries to arch again, but I'm met with resistance. Kylian maintains a hold on my neck, anchoring me to the blankets beneath me.

I reach for him with one hand, guiding him forward for a kiss.

He gives me what I want, bringing his mouth to mine, but I can barely return the slow, languid strokes of his tongue. All my focus is being monopolized by the man with his head buried between my thighs.

"Decker," I plead, gripping his hair with one hand and pulling him even harder against my core. He takes the opportunity to slide a single finger inside me, crooking it once against my G-spot, then rubbing back and forth against my inner wall once he hits the spot that makes me cry out.

He builds me up. He torments me with his mouth; with the grip on my thighs that seems to tighten every time Kylian squeezes my throat and the others caress my legs.

I feel them everywhere as my mind goes blank and my body soars.

"Decker. *Please*," I pant. "I'm so fucking close."

"Fuck, baby. I love to hear you beg. Say my name again."

His mouth reconnects with my core. A second finger slides inside, scissoring against my sweet spot in a torturous rhythm. When he sucks my clit hard and presses into my G-spot at the same time, I hit a stratospheric peak I've never crested before.

"Decker. Decker. *Decker*," I chant. Every syllable is a plea, my needy desperation for him so intense, I can't do anything but feel.

In that moment, I exist on two planes. I straddle the peak of pleasure, my orgasm still building as my four men send me higher and higher.

I'm wound so tightly, every muscle in my body burns.

I'm so far gone I forget to breathe, the oxygen deprivation adding to the heady, blurry edge of bliss.

"Come for me, Mrs. Crusade."

The command is followed by a sharp nip of his teeth.

I'm helpless to do anything but exactly what he says. I tip and fall, spiraling all the way down.

My body spasms, my pussy weeps in satisfaction. Tears leak from my eyes. My muscles go slack as every cell in my body rejoices in release.

Soothing words wash over me, four sets of hands grazing over my skin and holding me steady as the world tilts on its axis then rights itself once more.

Decker sits back on his knees, his gaze flitting from my face to my exposed, spasming sex. "We all want in tonight, Siren. Will you let us all in?"

"Yes," I consent with a shuddering, eager inhale. "Have me. Fill me. Fuck me and make me yours."

"Nicky's first," Kylian whispers in my ear.

My guys move around me, Decker taking the leg that Nicky was just holding as he shifts into position.

"Look at me, Hot Girl," Nicky encourages, dragging the tip of his dick through my folds. "I want your focus right here as I slide inside you and we break Decker's favorite rule together."

My initial snort transforms into a moan as he enters me. The angle is exquisite. I'm exposed in the most erotic way. I know the others' eyes are on us. But in this moment, all I see is my sweet Nicky.

"Right there," I encourage, loving the way he pounds into me at the perfect pace.

Kylian wraps his hand around my throat. Decker and Kendrick caress up my legs, holding me wide open.

"Nicky," I plead, not even sure what I'm asking for. I just want him. I need him so badly it hurts. The rest of our lives won't be long enough to show him all the ways I love him.

Knowing just what I need, he brushes at the guys' arms, and when they release me, he scoops me up so I'm sitting in his lap.

I savor the stretch. Surrender to the intimacy of being so deeply connected, mind, body, and soul. Seconds tick by. Water laps at the sides of the boat. Nothing else matters except this single moment where we're joined as one and he's holding me like he never wants to let me go.

As the emotion passes, my body craves more. Squirming in his lap, I grind my clit against his pubic piercing. I'll never grow tired of feeling the cool, smooth metal against my tight bundle of nerves.

"Plant your feet on either side of me, Hot Girl."

I do as I'm told, steadying myself and essentially hovering so just the first two inches of his length are sheathed inside me.

With a self-assured smirk, he lifts his hips, raises his pierced eyebrow, then waits for me to nod and give him the go ahead.

He fucks up hard, fast, and with impressive stamina, driving me higher, higher, and higher still until an orgasm rolls through me and sends me tumbling back into his lap.

Warmth coats my insides, Nicky's release blending with mine as we kiss and cuddle close.

It's not until Kylian's at my back that I even remember the others are here with us. When I scan the boat, three ravenous sets of eyes meet my gaze.

"My turn," Kylian declares, plucking me out of Nicky's lap.

Cum trickles down my thigh, but I know out of all my guys, Kylian cares the least about excessive liquids and cross-contamination. For a man who loves structure, he really does keep it fluid in our sex life.

"Lay on your side, baby. Legs together. Knees up."

It's as easy as breathing to take orders from this man. My body moves into position naturally, then Decker lifts my head and places a pillow beneath me. I'm deliciously cozy yet buzzing with anticipation as Kylian hovers and lines himself up.

One hand caresses my cheek, turning my head to face him.

Then he pushes in and wraps his hand around my throat all in one go. "Fucking perfect," he praises with a squeeze.

My pussy clenches around him, a weightless freedom washing over me as I surrender and let him take control.

He thrusts in deep, timing each roll of his hips with the curl of his hand.

"Look around, Jo. They love watching me take you like this, baby."

I can barely move, but out of the corner of my eye, I catch Decker's and Kendrick's laser-sharp focus on me. Their expressions are hungry, borderline feral. They both have their dicks in hand.

"Do you love when Daddy chokes you?" Kylian asks.

"I love it," I confirm, fighting to suck in enough oxygen as my vision blurs around the edges and everything else ceases to exist.

I love it. I need it. I crave it.

"Harder, Daddy," I beg.

He gives and gives. He knows my body so well that with a final thrust and a constricting squeeze, I come apart just for him.

Kylian is my safe place. In his hands I find pleasure; in his arms I find peace.

His devotion soothes all the frayed, broken edges I used to worry would never heal. I don't worry about healing or fixate on my past the way I used to. That's because of him, and all of them. They see me exactly as I am. They love me just like this.

"Are you with us, baby?" Kylian asks, running his nose along my jaw and tenderly kissing my neck.

"Ask again later," I tease. I'm so sated I could fall asleep right here.

"No magic eight ball answers, Mama." Kendrick scoops me up into his arms. "It's my turn, and if I don't get inside you right this fucking second, I'm going to embarrass myself in front of my boys."

Kendrick rolls me to my back and glides in with absolutely no resistance. I'm already wet and dripping from the others, but K doesn't seem to care. He drills into me, pushing the cum deeper and filling me fuller with each thrust.

"I fucking love you," he professes, holding himself above me and sensually driving his length deeper and deeper into my tight channel.

I was sated just moments ago. But Kendrick sparks a need inside me that only he can fill.

I smooth my fingers over his facial hair, pulling him to me and kissing him deeply before issuing my request. "Will you take my ass, K?"

His answering grin is all the confirmation I need. "With fucking pleasure. Flip over for me, Mama. Let me get you ready."

I mourn the loss of him the second he pulls out, but I know I'm going to be feeling even more full once he's fucking my other hole. Flipping to hands and knees, I stretch out my upper body. K grips both cheeks of my ass and squeezes, really digging in.

I hear him spit one second before the wad lands on my puckered hole.

Fuck. Yes. I love when he makes it filthy for me.

Fingertips brush my clit, then I'm surprised when two fingers push into my cunt. Before I can say anything, Kylian speaks up from behind us.

"Lube?"

He asks it as a question, but we all know it's a requirement for anal.

Kendrick crooks two fingers along my inner wall and drags them out slowly. There's clear amusement in his voice when he replies. "I mean, you and Nicky left me two loads to work with over here, Daddy Genius. Bring it over just in case, but I think I'm all set for now."

He paints my backdoor with warm cum before pushing one finger into me. The initial sting is quickly followed by the carnal urge I always feel when he plays with me back there. More. I want more. I want all of him, and I want it now.

Impatiently, I push back, fucking myself on the single digit he's given me so far.

"Relax, Mama. You know I'll get you there."

He's right. He's so fucking good to me. I exhale and stretch out again, letting my body relax as another finger breaches my hole. He fucks in and out a few times, quickly getting me to three.

"Breathe," he reminds me. "Open up, Jojo. You're doing so well for me. Let's show your boys how much you love getting fucked in the ass."

I squeeze around his fingers impatiently. He chuckles, removes his hand, and quickly coats his dick with lube.

He slaps the crown of his cock between my thighs—spanking my clit on the first few passes, then aiming so the slick head hits against my asshole in rapid succession.

I'm lost to the sensation when he breaches me.

"Breathe," he reminds me again, smoothing both hands up and down my bare back before settling them on my hips. "Let me in, Mama. Let me fuck you just how you like it."

I release a slow, steady exhale as Kendrick gradually drives into my ass. When he's buried to the hilt, I groan. It burns in the best way. It excites every nerve in my body, knowing the others are watching.

He eases in and out with measured thrusts, letting me fully adjust to the sensation.

"You're choking me, Mama. So fucking tight. So fucking good."

I preen at his praise, but I'm gripped by a deeper desire in the next breath.

I'm so full. It feels so good.

But I'm also still empty and aching.

With an uncertain, shaky breath, I turn my head and rest my cheek on the satin blanket below me.

On instinct, I search for Decker. He's just a few feet away, his expression both feverish and slack-jawed as his eyes dart from my face to where Kendrick's length disappears inside my body.

"I need you," I croak, unsure the words are even audible over the sound of all the moans and heavy breathing.

Decker's eyes go wide and his whole body locks up. At that moment, K hits that hard-to-reach spot deep inside, resulting in my pussy clenching around nothing and reminding me once more just how empty I truly am.

Fuck.

"Decker. *Please.*"

I look back over my shoulder, locking eyes with K. He knows the question before I even ask, his sly smile confirming that he's more than okay with what I'm craving right now.

"Yo. Daddy Genius," Kendrick calls out, slowing his thrusts in the process. "We're gonna need an assist."

Relief washes over me. I'm so blissed out I don't have enough brain cells to string together a coherent thought right now. I'm not about to try and explain the logistics of double penetration to the man who had rules about fornicating in open waters until a few hours ago.

"Let's lay back for him," Kendrick suggests. It shouldn't be so easy, but K lifts me up and keeps us connected, lying on his back while keeping his cock buried deep in my ass.

The new angle lights up all my nerve endings, making it impossible for me to fight against the urge to touch myself.

I run my hands up my legs, rubbing my clit several times before reaching lower. I caress around my gaping hole, massaging right where Kendrick's cock is stretching me wide. He groans behind me, gently thrusting up as I work us both over. I'm lost to the sensations, my eyes closed and my head tipped back to rest on Kendrick's chest.

Panting, I brush my hands up my torso, cupping my breasts, then squeezing my nipples to the point of pain.

No matter how hard I squeeze, and despite how full I already feel, something's missing. I know what it is. I just don't know if he's willing to give it.

When my lashes flutter open, I lock eyes with my husband. He's right there, staring down at me, his jaw ticking in determination, nodding every few seconds as Kylian talks low in his ear. We've done this once before, but not like this. I'm already so sensitive and swollen—he's going to have to fight to work his way in, especially at this angle.

He moves forward, cock in hand, stroking it slowly before dousing it with the lube Kylian provided.

Good call, Daddy Genius.

"This is what you want, Josephine?"

I tip my chin back proudly, letting him see my truth. "Yes. Fuck me, Decker. I want you to fill me all the way up while K fucks my ass."

With a shuddering breath, he lines himself up.

"Ease into it," Nicky encourages from the side.

Kendrick grunts. "Just get in here, Cap. You know how fucking good this is about to feel. She can take it."

Decker looks from my cunt to my face, worry emanating off him in waves. "You're sure?"

I bristle at his hesitation. I don't know who he thinks he's asking. Yes, I'm fucking sure. He needs to put it in. Right fucking now.

"Easy," Kendrick soothes, his hands running down my sides until his fingertips find my clit. I instantly relax, grateful for his touch. He always knows what I need, sometimes even before I do.

"I'll hold her still," Kendrick promises. "Slow and steady, but when you feel resistance, just keep going. I swear she can take it, Cap. She wants you. She needs her husband right now."

That does it.

Decker fumbles on the first few attempts, but once he's in, he's fucking in.

"Yes. Fuck. Right there, Decker. Yes."

He drives deeper, steadying himself with one hand on my hip while the other seeks out my center.

Both men play with me, Kendrick using two fingers to hold open my folds while Decker rolls my clit between his forefinger and thumb.

I glance down and gasp. Their touch sends me soaring. But the sight of their hands working together has me clenching every muscle and teetering on the edge.

"Fuck, Mama. Not yet. He needs to be all the way in. Let him fucking have you."

I release a shaky exhale, desperate to stave off the orgasm threatening to pull me under.

"Fuck. So tight, Siren. You feel so fucking good."

"Do you need more lube?" Kylian asks.

Decker grunts a sound of dismissal. "I've fucking got her."

Then he spits on my clit, and I fucking lose it.

My body convulses and spasms, the orgasm unleashing all the tension and reservedness both men exhibited up until this point.

"Push in when I pull out, Cap. Think about fucking up into her."

Decker nods once, quickly meeting the rhythm K sets.

Every few seconds, my inner walls clench so tightly I lock one of them in place. But they're relentless. Persistent. Determined and so fucking stubborn.

The next orgasm builds fast. The pressure is almost too much to bear. I can't hold back, and more importantly, I don't want to. Not now. Not ever again.

My eyes water as the urge builds in my core.

This isn't just an orgasm. It's about to be a baptism.

"K," I whimper, my mind already buzzing as my legs start to shake.

"Fuck yeah," Kendrick murmurs. "Keep it up, Cap. Your wife's about to squirt. Once it starts, don't you dare fucking stop. Just keep fucking her through it."

Decker's eyes flare with panic. I reach out and grip his neck, bracing myself for the deluge that's about to take hold.

"It feels so good," I assure him.

Warmth washes over me. Electricity zaps up my thighs. I dig my nails into Decker's scalp and lock eyes with my husband as a gush of fluid bursts from my pussy and absolutely soaks him.

"Don't stop, don't stop," I chant, throwing my head back against K's chest and pinching my nipples again.

Mouths descend on me as Kylian and Nicky move my hands and suck on my tits. They're anything but gentle—tugging and biting with such ferocity I throb all the way down in my core.

"One more, Mama. We're all here for you. We want this as much as you do. Give us one fucking more."

Kylian presses two fingers into my mouth, then moves that hand down to my clit. That would be enough, honestly, but then I feel another hand. And another. And another.

They're all touching me—working together like the perfect team to push me toward the final release.

My mind succumbs. My body submits. I scream and gush and absolutely drench them all, squirting more and spasming harder than I ever have in my life.

Serenity settles over me as I fade in and out of cognizance. That may have been the hottest group sex ever, but somehow, I also feel unbelievably cherished in this moment. I drift off to sleep for a few minutes, coming to with an even deeper sense of love and appreciation for my four amazing men.

Decker and Kendrick have pulled out, and Nicky is gently cleaning me up. Kylian strokes my hair, whispering words of admiration and praise.

Decker and Kendrick separate the wet blankets from the useable ones, laying everything out around us and rearranging the pillows.

Emotion clogs my throat as I watch them work together. Kylian guides me over and lays me down on the fresh blankets. I snuggle up against them, feeling more settled and satisfied than I ever have in my life.

Nicky lies near my left leg, planting a sloppy kiss on my stomach and grinning up at me before mouthing "love you" and wrapping a tatted hand around my thigh.

Kylian situates himself so he's up near my head, his lips at my ear. He keeps praising me, the steady stream of veneration warming me from the inside out.

Kendrick smooths his big palm up the length of my right leg, coming to rest with his stubbled jaw pressed into my side. I reach down and scratch his head, delighting when he closes his eyes with a satisfied smile.

Decker finally joins us, weaving his arm under my head and possessively grabbing one of my breasts. The cool underside of his wedding band brushes against my nipple and inspires a full body shiver.

Peering up at him, I wait until I catch his gaze.

"Thank you," I tell him softly.

For tonight. For this life. I couldn't even begin to properly thank any of them for everything they've done for me. For the love and security. For the hope and the joy.

I don't know what I did to deserve these men and the beautiful life we're creating. But as they surround me, each one snuggling close, touching me and peppering my skin with kisses all while whispering their adoration, I decide it doesn't matter. Everyone deserves the chance to live the truest, fullest, most beautiful version of their life.

It's me and them, forever and ever. I'll never take for granted the way we all care for one another.

I am here. This is now.

This is my happily ever after. I plan to hold on tight and never let it go.

Afterword and Acknowledgments

Something magical happened while I was writing So Right (Boys of South Chapel book four). That story prominently features the characters from my previous series, Boys of Lake Chapel, so I assumed it would be fun to revisit Joey and her cohort. Anyone who knows me knows that I can't do things halfway. I only play full out. Once I started writing about Joey and her boys again I wasn't satisfied just writing *about* them. I wanted to write more *for* them, if that makes sense.

Being back at the Crusade Mansion altered my brain chemistry somehow. Even after I finished the Boys of South Chapel series, I couldn't think of anything else besides writing something new for the Lake Chapel crew. Stats Daddy, Cap, Emo Boy, and K are all comfort characters for me, just like I know they are for many of you. I started dreaming about what if... and then the idea for Too Sweet was born.

I'm very into the woo, so when the Universe wouldn't leave me alone about these characters, I knew it was a sign to give you more. More swoony moments, spicy scenes, and character growth. More easter eggs, inside jokes, and over-the-top grand gestures. AND DON'T EVEN GET ME STARTED on Decker's floating love nest. Making Cap finally break his boat sex rule just might be the highlight of my career!

I was fortunate to commission **Oli D** to create a custom illustration for the boat scene (which you can view on Patreon or purchase in my Etsy Shop). **Silver from Bitter Sage Designs** was available to create a gorgeous new cover (which is honestly my favorite in the series!). Joey's struggles and the entire plot for this novella flowed out of me so easily. It was almost like she needed this book to help her heal. Everything came together seamlessly for Too Sweet. In the end, I think this is how it was always meant to be.

This novella is the product of a dream, but it was only possible because of the amazing team around me who said HELL YES when I told them we were going to do back-to-back releases, just two weeks apart. Special thanks to **my Megan** (not to be confused with all the other Megans out there...) and to **my bestie and editor Beth** who both played essential roles in making Too Sweet a reality. And of course, all the love and appreciation for **Mr. Abby**, who held it down at home and held me together while I pushed to get this project done on time.

I hope you loved being back with Joey and her guys as much as I loved writing them again. On to the next!

Also By Abby Millsaps

The Hampton Hearts series:
interconnected standalone small town romance novels

Golden Boy
Mr. Brightside
Fourth Wheel
Full Out Fiend

The Boys of Lake Chapel:
a why choose sports romance series

Too Safe: Boys of Lake Chapel Book One
Too Fast: Boys of Lake Chapel Book Two
Too Far: Boys of Lake Chapel Book Three
Too Sweet: Boys of Lake Chapel Novella

The Boys of South Chapel:
a why choose second chance romance series

So Wrong: Boys of South Chapel Book One
So Real: Boys of South Chapel Book Two
So Rare: Boys of South Chapel Book Three
So Right: Boys of South Chapel Book Four

About The Author

Abby Millsaps is an author and storyteller who's been obsessed with writing romance since middle school. In eighth grade, she failed to qualify for the Power of the Pen State Championships because "all her submissions contained the same theme: young people falling in love." #LookAtHerNow

She's best known for writing unapologetically angsty romance that causes emotional damage for her readers. Creative spicy scenes and consent as foreplay are two hallmarks of her books. Abby prides herself in writing authentic characters while weaving mental health, chronic illness, and neurodiverse representation into the fabric of her stories.

Connect with Abby
Website: www.authorabbymillsaps.com
Patreon: https://www.patreon.com/AbbyMillsaps
Instagram: @abbymillsaps
TikTok: @authorabbymillsaps
Email: authorabbymillsaps@gmail.com
Newsletter: https://geni.us/AuthorAbbyNewsletter
Facebook Reader Group: Abby's Full Out Fiends

www.ingramcontent.com/pod-product-compliance
Lightning Source LLC
LaVergne TN
LVHW030323070526
838199LV00069B/6542